Silent Night, Unholy Night

Refugee Stories

Sandra Saccucci, PH.D.

"Don't act like the hypocrite
Who thinks he can conceal his wiles
By loudly quoting the Koran"

Hafez, 14th Century Persian Poet

Contents

Silent Night, Unholy Night

"MY HUSBAND WOULD say to me all the time, "You're as smart as the tip of my penis." A cloud of incredulity enveloped me. I had never heard of such a cruel and chauvinistic expression in my entire life. I was revolted to the point of nausea. That statement underscores the psychology of men who abuse women, including their wives, girlfriends, spouses, sisters and other female relatives. The statement smacks of sexism and accentuates the physical and emotional nature of domestic violence. This woman had been degraded and demeaned by her husband for the duration of her marriage – two decades. Her name was Adobe. She was a tall, heavy-set woman, with short, curly black hair and jet black, beautiful eyes. Her country of origin was Nigeria.

Adobe proceeded to state, "One day he returned from his work and he demanded to know why his dinner was not hot enough. I put it onto the hot plate, but still, he didn't think it was hot enough. I told him I was really tired from cooking, cleaning and caring for our children. We had three young children then and I was also pregnant. He didn't want to hear it. He shouted his orders to me as if I were one of his soldiers.

He was a high ranking military officer in the Nigerian Army. 'Make the tea, bitch,' he demanded."

"I made the tea. But, it took too long. So, he poured the boiling water on my leg."

"I screamed in pain. It really hurt. I ran outside to get some help. One of our neighbors took me to the local hospital. The doctor took care of me. He asked me what happened, and when I told him, he gave me a dirty look as if I was annoying him. He pretended he didn't hear me. That's the way it is in Nigeria."

"I had to stay overnight, but the next day I went home. I didn't want to go home, but I had nowhere else to go. I fed my children, took care of them and then went to bed. Later on that night, my husband came home in a bad mood. He started shouting at me, 'Who the hell do you think you are, lying to the doctor about me?' I responded, 'I didn't lie.'

"I shouldn't have said that."

"I should have kept my mouth shut. You'd think by then I would have learned this lesson. I was stupid. I am stupid. I didn't go to school. My dad was poor, and anyway, he didn't think school was important for a girl. He sold me to my husband to pay off a debt he owed him. I was only 14 years old, just a child. My mom was against it, but she didn't matter to my dad."

"I tried to be a good wife, but it was hard. My husband would bring home girls and he would have sex with them right in our own home. He even forced me to make them tea afterwards. I didn't want to make the tea, but I knew that if I didn't, I would get a beating. Sometimes, I would spit in the tea. I'm ashamed of that. But all of us women did that."

At this point, my incredulity compelled me to intercede, "Your father sold you to repay a debt?"

"Yeh, that's common in my country," she replied in a matter-of-fact manner." Subsequently, she resumed her story as if her comment regarding her father was "normal."

"Over the years, I stopped feeling anything anymore. I was numb. Many days my husband would tie me with a chain so that I would not go outside. He thought I would have an affair. Can you believe that? I wasn't allowed to say, 'Are you kidding me? You don't even bother to hide your whores. You bring them home!' I had no rights whatsoever. It didn't matter to him that I was his wife. He hated me. I really didn't know why he even married me. What was the point? I guess he wanted a slave at home to cook and clean for him. I hated him. But, there was nowhere to turn. I knew of so many women like me. Many of our women are beaten by their husbands."

"One night I went into labor. I knew there was no point in asking my husband to take me to the hospital."

I asked, "What do you mean? You were carrying his baby. He should have taken you to the hospital."

"No, my husband never took me to the hospital when I went into labour with any of our children. That's just the way he is, and anyway, I didn't expect him to."

"Do you realize what you just said? He is your husband. This is his child. It's a given: he should be there for you emotionally, especially when you're delivering his child."

She just laughed, but it was a *hollow,* enervated laugh devoid of energy and spirit. Her husband had effectively "hollowed" her out.

"I called my dad. He took me to the hospital, although he wasn't too happy about it. Later on, my husband came to the hospital. He puts on a pretty good show in front of people. He's a good actor. He came into the birthing room with me. I was in a lot of pain. It was a slow labor. I wasn't in very good shape. I was really tired and sick from the beatings. But, of course, I couldn't blame him – at least not out loud. I asked him, 'Can you just hold my hand?' I didn't want *him* to comfort me, but I had no one else who would. He said, 'Here, I'll bring you a chair. Hold on to that.' So, he brought me a wooden chair. Something inside of me wouldn't let me hold onto that chair. I didn't know what it was. But, I refused to hold on to it, and instead thought, 'You can go to hell.'

At this point in her recollection, I was shocked by her husband's lack of human emotion toward his own wife, who is delivering his baby. He was as devoid of human compassion and empathy as the wooden chair he handed his wife in lieu of his own hand. What husband wouldn't hold his wife's hand during labor? What kind of a monster was this man? I was in awe of this woman. How could she have survived this kind of emotional and physical abuse? So, I asked her, "How did you endure this?"

"I had no choice."

"Why didn't you go to the police when he beat you?"

"Are you kidding? They wouldn't help me. He's a military officer with a lot of power. He's high up there. If I went to the police, he would find out, and beat me even more. I have children I have to raise. Who would raise my children if he killed me - one of his whores?"

I just sat there speechless, struggling to process all this information. As a woman, I was deeply disturbed and profoundly outraged.

"Did you talk to anyone, to a friend, a sister, a mother?"

"In the beginning, yeh, I told my family. But over time,

they didn't want to hear it anymore. They had their own problems. My dad hit my mom. My sisters were beaten up by their husbands too. I wasn't allowed to have friends, and anyway, abuse is common in Nigeria. If a woman complains, she is seen as dishonoring her husband. Women who suffer in silence are respected. 'Oh, she's a saint', people say. But a woman who complains is a bitch. Somehow it's her fault."

"If you did go to the police, would they write a Police Report?"

"Everyone knows they wouldn't. Anyway, it's legal to hit your wife in Nigeria."

"Wait a second, you can't be right. It's actually legal, lawful to abuse your wife in Nigeria? It's not considered an assault, a criminal offence? What does your Criminal Code state?"

"I don't know nothing about any code. All I know is that men hit their wives and it's not a crime."

At this juncture, I made a note to myself, "Research the Criminal Code in Nigeria. Is wife battery a criminal code offence? Is it considered an assault?"

Unfortunately, she was right. Section 55(1) of the Penal Code Law No. 18 of 1959 (Cap 89, 1963 Laws of Northern Nigeria), states:

"Nothing is an offence which does not amount to infliction of grievous hurt upon any person and which is done by a husband for the purpose of correcting his wife, such husband and wife being subject to any native law or custom in which such correction is recognized as lawful."

… According to Section 24 of the Penal Code, "grievous hurt" is defined as,

"Permanent loss of sight, ability to hear or speak, facial disfigurement, deprivation of any member or joint, bone fracture or tooth dislocation, and other endangering harm."

Additionally, law enforcement agents practice a policy of non-interference in domestic violence cases, and reportedly regard a certain degree of physical battery as culturally acceptable. According to custom and social ethos, women who do have the courage to seek state protection are often viewed as insubordinate and disobedient towards their husbands and antithetical to cultural and societal norms. In short, these women are viewed as social outcasts. It is no wonder then that abused women, including Adobe, adopt a culture of silence. Further, marital rape is unrecognized by law in Nigeria because consent to marriage is tantamount to consent to sexual intercourse whenever a husband pleases and regardless of his wife's will.

So, according to section 55 of the Penal Code in the Northern States, it is perfectly acceptable for a man to hit a female relative as a means of disciplining or correcting her "bad" behavior as long as he does not cause grievous hurt. So, this means that it is lawful for a man to punch his wife, kick her, pull her hair, give her black eyes, spit at her and so on. Moreover, it is lawful for a man to rape his wife because, in effect, she already consented to sexual intercourse at any time, in any circumstance, regardless of her own will, when she entered into marriage.

I was truly flabbergasted to the point where I had to read these sections of the Penal Code over and over again. I thought, "This can't be right." I had difficulty in wrapping my mind around this legislation. But, there it was in clear language. I called a colleague and discussed the legislation. She too was flabbergasted. The two of us shared our moral outrage.

After the telephone call, I sat silently at my desk for an hour, unable to move. Then, I became angry. This was a good thing. It motivated me. This anger compelled me to want to help this woman and advocate for her as strongly as I could. I channeled that anger into doing just that. She was much more to me than just a client. She was an individual whom touched my heart.

Adobe had such a horrible life. No one would help her despite the fact that they knew the extent of the abuse her husband was inflicting on her. Her own family turned their backs on her. She deserved to have someone in her life who genuinely cared about what happened to her, who genuinely wanted to be there for her. So, I poured my heart into her file.

"How did you eventually leave Nigeria? What was the last straw?" I asked her.

"What do you mean?"

"Well, why did you finally leave?"

"Oh, it was my daughter, my oldest daughter, Yoruba, who's with me here in Canada. My husband came after her. She was just trying to help me. See, one night, he brought home a girl my daughter's age. It made my daughter sick to her stomach. She couldn't take it anymore. She told me, "Mom, please, do something. I don't want to see this." So, I told my husband, "I know you hate me, but what about our daughter? Do you hate her too? Can't you see how upset she is? For God's sake, take the girl someplace else. What, you can't afford a room some place?"

'Listen, bitch, he said, 'it's my money, not yours. When

you make some money, then you can say something, and good luck, you're too stupid to work. You should be grateful I put a roof over your head. Your father sold you to me – that's how much he loves you.' He laughed. He actually laughed. But you know what hurt me the most?"

"He was right. My dad didn't love me. I was nothing to him. He did sell me to my husband."

"Unfortunately, many victims of domestic violence are pre-scripted for that life because they didn't feel loved as children – indeed; they were not loved as children. They didn't receive the kind of love which makes us strong, which makes us set boundaries for ourselves as women. I think a father's love is so critical to a girl and her future. It sets the tone for us as women, for our ability to set boundaries, and not allow men to hurt us. You didn't have that from your own father."

"Yeh, my dad didn't love me, but my poor mother did. She was just too beaten down to show it."

"Yes, this is also common with victims of domestic violence. Often, they come from homes wherein their mothers are abused, and this becomes a vicious circle. Mothers are abused, and consequently, their daughters are abused."

"Yeh, you see that a lot in my country."

"What happened next?"

"My husband punched me in the stomach and began beating me. Our daughter tried to get in between us. So, he beat her senseless. I screamed for help. No one came, and I know our neighbors heard the screams. It was a silent night, an unholy night. No one wants to get involved in Nigeria. They just ignore beatings, screams. No one really cares. So, I carried my daughter in a wheelbarrow all the way to the hospital. She was seen by a doctor. He treated her, but he asked no questions. He didn't care. He just took care of her wounds. Again, it seemed as if my daughter and I were annoying him."

"My daughter was kept overnight. I stayed with her. The next day, we went home. I told my daughter not to say a word to her father and that I would try and figure a way out."

"So, that was the triggering event, right?"

"What?"

"I mean, that's what caused you finally to leave Nigeria, correct?"

"Yeh, my daughter."

"So, it's sad in a way, don't you think? I mean, you knew that your husband's beating of your daughter was wrong, but you endured his abuse of you for years. Why didn't you think you were good enough to save?"

"Me, no. What's so good about me? I'm old, fat, ugly, stupid, poor - who would want me?"

"That's not true. You're none of those things. Your husband has brainwashed you into thinking about yourself in that manner. I see a kind, selfless, sweet and extremely brave woman, who endured hell for years and still survived. I mean, it took courage for you to leave Nigeria and come here to a foreign country. It took courage for you to bring your daughter."

"I was scared, for me and for my daughter. But, I couldn't let him start hitting her, like he did to me. I just couldn't watch that. It made me sick, really sick. My health started to get worse. It was killing me. I knew that if I stayed, I would probably end up dead. What good would I be to my children then? No, I could at least save my oldest."

"Where are your other children?"

"In Nigeria. I couldn't take them with me."

At this point, she began to cry. As a mother myself, I

shared her agony. No mother can leave her children behind, unless she is forced to do so. She cried for quite some time. This poor woman needed to share her grief, and I was touched that she was sufficiently comfortable with me to do so. That meant I was doing my job.

After a respectable period, I asked her, "Are you O.K.?"

"Sorry, I never do that. Sorry."

"There's no need to apologize. You went through hell and back. It's amazing that you're actually here in this room, telling me your story. You're stronger than your husband has led you to believe. See, men who abuse their wives are strategic: they are able to get away with the physical and emotional abuse because they isolate their wives so that the women lose perspective. You kept telling me that the abuse is 'normal', but it's anything but 'normal.'" It's not acceptable. The real tragedy with abused women is not the physical harm because bruises heal over time. The real tragedy is the emotional harm because abused women internalize the abuse and consequently, they don't see themselves as worthy of love."

"Worthy of love? Of course, I'm not worthy of love. Look at me. What man would want me?"

"No, that's your husband's voice. He's wrong. Any man would be fortunate to have someone as ethical, strong and beautiful as you in his life."

"No… I'm not beautiful. You know what? My husband never once looked at me when he took me to bed – not once. He would take me from behind."

"I'm afraid I don't understand."

"He never faced me or looked at me when he had sex with me. He would have sex with me by turning my back to him and putting me against the wall. There was no kissing, no hugging, no touching - just straight intercourse. The whole thing would last just a few minutes. That's it."

"I am so sorry. That's degrading and dehumanizing to you as a woman and you didn't deserve that – no woman does. That's just plain wrong. Where did he learn to make love – no, I correct myself: that's not making love."

"I heard that the first time he had sex was when he was just a teenager. He went to a prostitute."

"Yes, that makes sense because the manner in which he had sex with you is like having sex with a prostitute: there is no love, no intimacy, no humanity, or commitment. What your husband did to you in bed is truly sick and revolting. You must have felt dehumanized, yes?"

"Yeh, I felt like a prostitute – that's true. I felt like one of his whores. I was desperate for a kind hug, a kind word, a kind touch. I was starving. So, I ate. I ate and ate and ate. See, look at how fat I am. It's disgusting. He's right about me. I'm disgusting."

"No, you're anything but disgusting. You're a beautiful woman, and a great mother. The reason you overate is because you were emotionally starved. This is actually common for many abused women. However, now, you can begin to reclaim your own body, yes? You can eat properly, exercise and take care of yourself – love yourself."

"I hate myself."

"Yes, you hate yourself now. That's because you've internalized the abuse: you've internalized your husband's hatred of you. There was nowhere else for you to channel that abuse. The police, the doctors, your neighbors, and your own father – indeed, your entire society would not help you. You certainly couldn't voice your anger to your husband because that would result in a beating. But, you had to do something with that anger. So, you ate. I understand that."

"Yeh, and I was never once satisfied in my marriage."

"What do you mean?"

"I never had an orgasm, not once."

"Well, that's because your husband didn't make love with you. That would entail actually caring about your needs, including your need, as a woman, to be sexually satisfied. He was only concerned with his own crude, barbaric and animalistic sexual needs. Your husband has no idea of how to treat a woman. Why do you think he had sex with prostitutes?"

"Because they're skinny and young."

"No, Adobe, that's what he wanted you to believe. In my view, he had sex only with prostitutes because he has a distorted and sick view of women. Women mean nothing to him. He demeans and degrades them, and then he disposes of them, like one would dispose of garbage. Your husband is a sick and disgusting man."

"One time, he brought a girl home. He took her into our bedroom. He had her. Then, he came into the kitchen and got some liquor. He barked orders at me, 'Get two nice glasses, the expensive ones I was good enough to buy you.' I don't drink, and so that didn't even make sense to me. I gave him the glasses. I felt sick inside when I did that. But, I had no choice. If I refused, he would beat me. My kids were sick and tired of the beatings."

"My husband and his girl drank together and got drunk. Afterwards, when I wanted to go to sleep, he said to me that his girl was sleeping in our bed. I should sleep somewhere else. I told him he should drive her home. That was the decent thing to do. The kids were upset to see her in their home. He said, 'I'm too drunk. So, the girl stays.'

"I am so sorry for you and your children."

"Thank you. So, in the morning, the girl got up. The children and I were having breakfast. She demanded, 'Make me toast and tea, bitch.' Can you believe that?"

"What did your husband say or do?"

"Where do you think she got the guts to talk to me that way?"

"Your husband gave her license to speak to you in that manner."

"Yeh, but my kids were upset and they all looked at me. So, I said, 'No, get out. You're upsetting my kids.' That was a big mistake."

"Why?"

"My husband beat me in front of the children. There was blood everywhere. My kids were crying and screaming for him to stop. His girl just smiled. So, I cleaned myself up, and made her the tea and toast."

At this point, I felt nauseated. I excused myself and ran into the bathroom, where I proceeded to vomit. Lawyers are trained to be professional, objective, matter of fact and unemotional. We are trained in this manner for many reasons, including, but not limited to the fact that if we become emotionally invested in each and every client, eventually and inevitably, we will burn out.

However, lawyers are also human beings, and the abuse she described made me sick as a woman. Further, I have always been of the opinion that lawyers who truly feel for their clients are better and stronger advocates because we are able to present their stories through their eyes.

After I cleaned myself up, she looked at me and asked, "Are you O.K.?" I thought this poor woman has suffered immeasurably, and yet, she still has the milk of human kindness in her: she is actually concerned about me. I responded, "I'm fine. Continue with your story."

"My husband drank a lot, and every time he drank, he would beat me. I would say to him, 'You're Muslim - you're not even allowed to drink.'

'He would say, 'You call yourself a good Muslim wife? I know you go behind my back and tell people lies about me.'

'What lies?, I asked.'

'You tell people I hit you. You dishonor me and our kids. You should be ashamed of yourself.'

'But, you *do* beat me', I said.

'You're a liar. People laugh at you. They don't believe you. They make fun of you and feel sorry for me to be stuck with such a wife. They respect me. They hate you. Everyone does, even your own father.'

"Then he punched me over and over again in the face."

"Oh, my God. He is sadistic, misogynistic – pure evil."

"Yeh, I don't know what that means, but yeh, he's bad."

At this point, both of us broke out into bubbles of laughter. We couldn't help ourselves. We didn't share a perfect language of communication, but we shared something else – we shared an emotional language of connection. That's why we laughed, and it was healthy for her and for me. The interview was emotionally intense and enervating for both of us. She cried, and I felt like crying – only, I didn't think it professional. Nonetheless, this exchange of laughter seemed to provide the emotional nourishment she required to continue relaying her painful and heart-wrenching story. But, before she did so, she asked, relaying her painful and heart-wrenching story. But, before she did so, she asked,

"Do you have kids?"

"Yes."

"So, as a mother, you understand how hard it was for me to leave my other kids behind?"

"That would be like ripping out my heart."

"Thank you for saying that. You know, you're the first person to ever say that to me? That's means so much to me. The other lawyers I went to didn't say that to me."

"You have one daughter with you, so there's hope. Hold on to that. How did you manage to leave Nigeria with her?"

"Our imam helped me. He was a good man, married with children. He didn't hit his wife. So, he helped me. He got us Visitors' Visas to see my cousin here in Windsor. I got to take my daughter, but he said Immigration wouldn't let me take all my children with me. They would think I wasn't coming back to Nigeria. Plus, my husband wouldn't have allowed it."

I knew she meant the Canadian Consulate had the discretion to not grant Visitors' Visas for her and all of her children if they believed they would not return to Nigeria on the expiry date of the visas. To be granted a Visitor's Visa she would have to prove, among many things, permanent ties to her country of origin, including the presence of children back home.

A pronounced question mark mirrored my client's eyes.

"What is it?" I asked her.

"Well, do I have to talk about the beatings in court?" she inquired.

"Of course, you do. You have to tell your story. That is what the refugee hearing is all about."

"I don't think I can."

"Why not?"

"Because a good woman doesn't tell on her man."

I was outraged by this line of manipulation fed to so many women in various countries. Good women suffer domestic violence in silence in order to protect their family honour. Only "bad" women disclose violence at the hands of their male relatives, partners and husbands. So, suffering in silence is re-defined as a virtue, when in reality, it is a self-serving device used by batterers to perpetuate the abuse. I had heard this false rhetoric in the language of domestic violence ad nauseum, and it sickened me each time I heard it.

This rhetoric of abuse is analogous to the same flawed logic wife batterers use in order to justify the abuse. The argument goes, "you provoked me. It's your fault I hit you. If you would just change I wouldn't hit you anymore." I had heard this weak line of argumentation repeatedly for over a decade. The onus of responsibility for the abuse is displaced onto the woman: it's her fault she is abused and if she discloses the violence, it is a reflection of her bad character. The simple truth is: abuse is a reflection of the abuser's character and not his victim's character. However, abused women are so profoundly indoctrinated, so silenced that it is extremely difficult for them to speak about the abuse to anyone, let alone in a public forum, such as a hearing.

In this vein, one of the biggest hurdles I had to assist my client in overcoming was to speak about the abuse at the refugee hearing and to trust that the panel member would not regard her as a "bad" woman for so doing. To this end, it assisted her immensely and immeasurably to discuss the abuse with me, with a woman she trusted. This trust took a great deal of time, and she would not have the luxury of time with respect to the panel member. Therefore, I decided to make a request to the Immigration and Refugee Board to reverse the order of questioning so that I could question her first rather than last. In this way, I would be able to elicit her story in a non-adversarial and gentle manner. Subsequently, the tribunal officer and/or the panel member could question her or seek clarification. The reverse order of questioning is highly effective with respect to gender persecution cases, including victims of domestic violence or human trafficking. I had used this technique a myriad of times and clients testified much better in this type of structure.

The day of the hearing finally arrived – two and a half years after we had filed Adobe's Personal Information Form with the Immigration and Refugee Board in Toronto. The Personal Information Form, also referred to by the acronym PIF, is the basis for the refugee claim proper, and Adobe's story was included in her PIF. The protracted delay in the hearing date had a profoundly adverse effect on my client. She was overwrought with the fear that she would be deported to Nigeria. Her husband kept calling her in Canada, and demanding she return home to her children. He also wanted his daughter, Yoruba back. He felt that she would become too Westernized, or in his own words, "a whore." I found his comment rather hypocritical given the fact that he experienced no moral discomfort in sleeping with whores. Adobe agreed.

She was terrified of the imminent hearing. I encouraged her to seek counseling with respect to domestic violence, but she was still uncomfortable discussing the abuse with anyone. Additionally, as she kept reiterating to me, "We Muslim women don't talk to counselors or anyone. It's shameful." As a human being, I understood Adobe's discomfort; however, as a lawyer, I cautioned her and advised her that she required objective proof regarding the abuse, and a letter from a counselor would certainly assist in this regard. She did not; she could not comply with my advice. I knew it would have an adverse effect on her case, and I advised her as much.

Of course, this proved one of the issues at the hearing. The panel member did ask her, "Why didn't you seek counseling of some sort for the alleged domestic violence? You did not see a social worker, a psychiatrist, a doctor – why not?"

Adobe simply replied, "It's shameful."

The panel member scrunched up her eyes with a marked expression of incredulity. I tried to explain to her as follows,

"When a victim of domestic violence leaves her country behind, she doesn't necessarily leave her emotional baggage behind. More often than not, she carries that with her to Canada. In the case at bar, as Adobe herself tried to explain, she was indoctrinated by her father first, then her husband, and indeed by her society at large, to believe that a "good" Muslim woman does not speak about the abuse because this will dishonor her family. Indeed, Madame Chair, we have provided objective evidence in support of our position that abused women in general, regardless of their religion, ethnicity, socio-economic status, education, or lack thereof, often experience difficulty in breaking the silence. We have documentary evidence with respect to the Human Rights Violations in Nigeria regarding women. There is no police protection for them. Doctors turn a blind eye to the abuse. Their society at large, tolerates the abuse. There is nowhere for these women to turn."

"But, counsel, the panel member interjected, she is in Canada now. Why didn't she afford herself the opportunity to seek counseling? Surely, you advised her to obtain evidence to support her refugee claim?"

"Again, Madame Chair, she has been so profoundly indoctrinated that she believes it is shameful to discuss the abuse with a counselor."

I could not discuss whether or not I had advised Adobe to seek counseling as this would be a violation of solicitor/client privilege.

"Well, that doesn't make sense to me. Her husband is the one who should be ashamed for abusing her. So, why is she so ashamed if she is speaking the truth?"

"Madame Chair, she *is* speaking the truth. She was abused by her husband for twenty years. Her father abused her mother. Her father sold her to her military officer/husband to repay a financial debt he owed him. That is how much value he placed on his own daughter. So, Adobe is the victim here. She has been taught that she would be shaming her family's honor if she broke the silence and spoke about the abuse. One cannot undo this harm overnight. It takes time to heal."

"Counsel, I want you to address the following issues to the claimant: Why doesn't she have a Doctor's Note? In addition, why didn't she go to the police and ask for assistance when she was beaten up?"

I looked at Adobe softly in an attempt to console her. She appeared extremely agitated and terrified. I tried to reassure her as much as I could. "Adobe," I asked, "why didn't you ask your doctor for a note when you visited him after the beatings?"

"The doctor would not give me such a letter. Nobody talks about beating a woman up. It's all covered up. He wouldn't help me."

At this point, the panel member intervened, "But surely

doctors in Nigeria must report crimes, such as assault on a woman?"

"No, not in my country, they don't."

"I see", the Panel Member stated with an air of skepticism.

"Madame Chair, as Adobe has testified, her husband beat her up badly after he found out she visited her doctor. So, it only made matters worse for her. Furthermore, I would refer you to Exhibit 6, namely Section 55 of the Penal Code in the Northern States, which objectively substantiates my client's testimony in the sense that wife battery is not regarded as a crime as long as the husband does not cause – and I quote – 'grievous hurt.'

"Alright, I can accept that, but why didn't she even try to seek police protection."

"Her husband is a high ranking officer in the military, and the police would certainly not protect her against him."

At this point, the panel member asked Adobe directly, "But you didn't even try to seek police protection for your beatings, did you? Further, you didn't even try to seek police protection after your husband beat his own daughter, did you? You also left behind what, four other children. So, you failed to protect your own children, correct?"

I wanted desperately to intercede and refer the panel member to the voluminous documentary evidence regarding the inadequacy of police protection for abused women in Nigeria. I also wanted to explain that even if Adobe had sought police protection, it would only make matters worse. Her husband would beat her more severely for "dishonoring" him, for damaging his reputation.

I wanted to explain that Adobe is the victim here, and that her comments regarding her failure to protect her own children, were, in a sense, re-victimizing the victim. However, I wouldn't dare articulate that concern because it would only alienate the Panel Member, and frankly, giving voice to that concern would not be wise.

In any event, I so wanted to blurt out, "Adobe tried to protect her children, but she had no support whatsoever. The police would not assist her. She could not take all of her children with her as they would not be granted Visitor Visas. We provided objective evidence to substantiate all of these facts. However, the panel member needed to hear Adobe's explanation. I knew I would be given the opportunity to make oral observations later on.

"Your Honor," she began, "I didn't go to the police because I was too afraid. If my husband found out, he would beat me bad. He's a military man. The police won't help the wife of a military man. He has a lot of respect in my country. I tried to protect my children, especially my oldest daughter, Yoruba. My husband beat her too. The imam helped me get her a Visitor's Visa to Canada. But, he said Immigration wouldn't give all of my kids a Visitor's Visa. Why else could I do?"

At this point, she broke down and cried, and cried and cried. To be honest, I cried as well. I tried not to. I hid my tears from the Panel Member because I knew it wasn't professional. So, I lowered my head, and the Panel Member did not see my tears.

I was immensely frustrated. I had known Adobe for circa three years. I knew she was telling the truth. However, it would take a few short hours for one single Panel Member to assess her credibility – a few short hours – that's it. I had provided voluminous objective evidence regarding gender persecution, namely domestic violence in Nigeria, material on the lack of police protection, the lack of shelters for abused women, reports on the psychology of abused women, objective substantiation from reputable sources, including Country, Department of State, Amnesty International and Human Rights Watch Reports. I had gone way beyond the call of duty, particularly for a Legal Aid file which, as any lawyer knows, is purely a labor of love because one does not make money on a Legal Aid file; on the contrary, one loses money.

"Well, the panel member continued with her questioning, "you could have moved to a different location in Nigeria. Did you even try to?"

"No, I had no money, no education. Where was I to go?"

"Where did you get the money to come to Canada?"

"The imam gave me the money."

"So, why didn't you ask him to give you the money to re-locate you and your children away from your husband?"

"My husband would find us wherever we went to in Nigeria. He's in the military. Plus, how would I support my children? I have no schooling, no skills."

"I understand. Now, I want to ask you about your other children, namely, why did you leave them behind in Nigeria? If your husband was so abusive, it stands to reason that you would not leave them in his care, yes? It is not in their best interests, correct?"

"I had no choice. Immigration wouldn't give them visas. And I had to get out of there. I did the best I could."
The panel member appeared pensive for a long pregnant pause. Then, suddenly, she simply stopped questioning Adobe and requested oral observations. I would have preferred written observations because I sensed she was not likely to render a pos-

itive decision. I asked for Adobe's instructions as to this issue.

"I've had enough. Just say them out loud. I can't take it any-more. Not knowing whether Yoruba and I can stay in Canada is too stressful. I need this all to end. I knew the judge wouldn't believe me."

"I believe you."

"Well, that's something. That means something to me."

After a succinct 15 minute recess, I delivered my oral observations. They were lengthy and thorough. I advocated from the heart and substantiated every single comment with as much objective evidence as I could. There was ample objective evidence which supported Adobe's story. However, so much of a claim rests on subjective credibility, and the panel member assesses whether or not a claimant is telling the truth. Adobe testified in a forthright manner. She did not embellish her claim whatsoever. She was appropriately emotional without being melodramatic or engaging in disingenuous displays of drama.

However, she did hesitate in relaying her story. This was due to the fact that she was drained and enervated. She had waited for two and a half years for this hearing date. She was concerned about her other children back in Nigeria. She felt that the Panel Member was somehow blaming her for leaving behind her four other children. I tried to address all of these concerns in my oral observations. In the end, I too was exhausted. Adobe's story had indeed enriched my life, but it had also sucked the life out of me. This process is oxymoronic indeed and may be analogous to a pianist who plays her heart out. The music enriches her life, but playing it also sucks the life out of her.

The Panel Member reserved her decision. This was not a positive sign. It meant that she required time to think about the issues. She was not wholly convinced. I asked her if she required further written submissions from me. She responded simply, "No, you have provided amble objective evidence. I will render my decision as soon as possible.

"Madame Chair, how long do you expect to take?"

"I have a full plate. I will render a decision under the three months limit."

"Thank you, Madame Chair."

Two and a half months passed. Adobe was terrified of a negative decision. I was also concerned, and my concern grew exponentially as each day passed without receiving a decision. Finally, one day, my assistant advised the decision had arrived that morning. I ripped open the envelope and searched for the bottom line: positive or negative. I would read the decision carefully after knowing the outcome, the "verdict" as it were.

The panel member agreed that the objective evidence supported Adobe's refugee claim based on gender persecution. The difficulty she had was with Adobe herself, namely her credibility, and the lack of subjective evidence to support her claim. I had argued that Adobe did not feel comfortable seeking counseling in Canada because she had been indoctrinated that is was shameful to speak about her abuse. This would dishonor her family, including her husband. Adobe herself testified in the same vein. However, the panel member did not find this credible despite the objective documentary evidence. She was within her rights to do so. Unfortunately, Adobe could not provide any evidence from her siblings, mother or friends concerning the domestic violence she suffered at the hands of her husband. She tried to obtain such evidence, but unfortunately, no one would or could help her. Perhaps they were apprehensive of the repercussions from her husband - as I believed. Or perhaps, they simply did not care – as Adobe believed. Additionally, the Panel Member reasoned that her husband was not even present in Canada and therefore, she failed to understand how seeking counseling in Canada would dishonor him. She drew an adverse inference in terms of credibility because of this failure on Adobe's part to obtain proof of the abuse inside of Canada.

Of course, I wanted to appeal the decision, as well as to seek other immigration remedies, such as an Application for Permanent Residence on Humanitarian and Compassionate Grounds and a Pre-Removal Risk Assessment Application. Adobe was entitled to Legal Aid, and I wanted desperately to keep fighting for her and for her daughter, the next generation. However, Adobe, in her own words, "was tired, tired, tired."

She had no fight left in her. I did, but that did not matter anymore. It was wholly irrelevant.

She returned to Nigeria with her daughter, Yoruba. Sometime later, she actually managed to call me from Nigeria and we had a heart to heart discussion. Unfortunately, but not surprisingly, the cycle of abuse had come full circle: Adobe's husband continued to beat her, only more severely this time, after all she had fled to Canada and told her story, thereby dishonoring him. Yoruba couldn't stand to bear witness to her mother's abuse. She intervened. Consequently, her father beat her as well. Yoruba felt powerless to protect her mother. So, she did what many young girls in her situation do: she and her boyfriend ran off into the silent night and the two married shortly thereafter. The night, the unholy night would silence Yoruba just as it had her mother...

For shortly thereafter, Yoruba's husband began abusing her... and unfortunately, the narrative of domestic violence, the story of abuse, will perpetuate to Yoruba's own daughters, and their daughters, and their daughters.

Only this time, no one in Canada will hear them.

Infidel

NADIA YOUSIF ATTENDED my office one crisp, cool and colorful Spring day. I always loved the Season of Spring with its vibrant hues of sun kissed greens, browns, blues, yellows, reds, violets and oranges, the shades of Spring, the shades of Rejuvenation, the substance of Life. Nadia's face was a stark tableau in contrast to Spring: her face was more like Autumn as it reminded me of sapless leaves cascading from a tree, lifeless, listless - dead.

She was a rather heavy-set woman in her late 30's. One could see her hair had been dyed a boring brown as the roots were jet black and peppered with elderly white. She appeared much older than her chronological years. She appeared neglected – self-neglected. Her face was depleted of color and oxygen. She looked as if she was a chain smoker. I could imagine her smoking cigarette after cigarette as a form of self-flagellation. Certainly, the stench of tobacco, like an evil ghost, preceded her entry into my office. I hoped the evil ghost was not a premoni-tion of things to come. I wondered why she smoked so much.

I was about to find out.

"My name is Alex. How may I assist you today?" I asked.

"I need to make a refugee claim," she responded hoarsely, in a smoker voice.

"I see. On what basis do you need to make your claim?"

"Religion and the Woman Claim."

"Alright, I think you mean Membership in a Particular Social Group, that is, as a woman, and Gender Persecution."

"Yeh, that's right."

"Then tell me your story."

"O.K."

Nadia filled her strangulated lungs with as much oxygen as she could. She would need it to convey her terrifying story.

"Well, I'm Chaldean, Christian from Iraq."

"Sorry," I interjected, "but you stated you're Christian?"

"Yes."

"Then, why are you wearing the burka, a Muslim cover?"

At this point, long suppressed floodgates opened and Nadia wept uncontrollably, "I don't know. I don't know. I'm afraid to uncover."

I was duly confused. I represented a myriad of Chaldean Christians from Iraq. They were proud and excited to finally wear the Cross of Christ, or some other symbol of their faith so freely and openly in Canada. Many of my clients had been persecuted, raped, beaten, tortured and imprisoned based on their Christian faith. Many members of their families, parents and siblings, had been brutally murdered based on their religion.

I sensed Nadia was not prepared to unravel the mystery of the burka just yet, and I stated as much.

"Alright, we'll return to the burka when you're ready. For

now, just take a deep breath. We have time. Go on with your story. I'm listening."

Nadia struggled in relaying her story, a struggle reflected in her tear stained face, tears emanating from a deep well of sheer, unmitigated hell. "

"Well, I went to Baghdad University. As a student I lived with my aunt in Baghdad as the university was in the capital on Al Jadiriya Street. I graduated with a degree in languages, including English. I wanted to be a translator. I worked for an American company. I loved my work. But, the terrorists and Muslim extremists viewed me as a traitor because the company was from the USA. So, they decided to punish me in the worst way for a woman...."

"What do you mean?"

"I was kidnapped, imprisoned in a home, forced to marry, and raped, if you can call it rape when you're married."

"Did you consent to sexual intimacy with your husband?"

"God, no, the opposite."

"Then, under Canadian Law, you were raped despite the fact that you were married. Further, you were forced to marry and coercion invalidates a marital contract."

"Not with Muslims in Iraq."

"I know, but you're safe now. You're on Canadian soil."

"Thank God."

My heart went out to Nadia as it was abundantly clear that she was profoundly traumatized in Iraq, and further, that her trauma continued here in Canada. Despite the fact that she had fled Iraq, she carried her trauma with her, inside her head.

"I had to go into hiding. Then, the terrorists and Islamists came to my parents' home. They threatened them, my brothers and sisters with death if they didn't say where I was hiding.

They raped and then killed my younger sister, Zeina right in front of my parents. My mother is not right even now. You know we say you die a thousand deaths on earth before you finally die in the After Life. Well, my mom died a thousand deaths when she saw my sister get raped and then stabbed over and over and over again. I'll never forgive myself for this. It's my fault my sister's dead. I wanted a career and look at what happened to my little sister."

Nadia looked devastated and enervated. Nevertheless, she also looked determined to get her story out. This was a good sign.

"These Muslim extremists and terrorists view me as a collaborator of the Americans not only because of my work, but also because of my religion. I was unable to practise or even express my religious beliefs in Iraq for fear I would be harmed or even killed."

"You know, my parents used to be so proud of me because I was the first and only daughter to graduate from university. But now, they are ashamed of me."

"Why would they be ashamed of you, Nadia?" I was perplexed.

"I dishonored my family. I was raped by a radical Muslim man."

"Nadia, *you* did not dishonor your family; the man who raped you did."

"Yeh, well, anyway, after my graduation, my friend, Kamil told me about a job prospect with an American company. This company had a contract with the USA Department of Defense. I was so excited about this job. I attended the interview in February 2004 and I was hired as a translator. This was my first job after graduating from university. The company's headquarters were in the Baghdad Hotel and I translated from inside the headquarter offices. I would travel to the outskirts of Baghdad and to other cities to help contractors and other personnel with translation. My father was worried about my safety as a woman; but, I was ambitious and I wanted to work. You see, in Iraq men are more ambitious than women, but I was different. And look where it got me?"

"Nadia, you keep blaming yourself for your positive attributes, including the fact that you earned an education and worked in your chosen field. There's nothing wrong with that; in fact, the opposite, it's commendable, particularly because, as you stated, women in Iraq are not as encouraged as men to study and pursue a career."

"Yeh", Nadia responded but without conviction or confidence. "Anyway," she continued, "I was assigned to work at Al Rusafa Prison, and during one of these assignments, I recognized one of the prisoners, Muhammad. We went to the same university. I saw him for awhile as a boyfriend, but I never slept with him. He was surprised when I said "no" because he thought Christian girls were different than Muslim girls. I explained to him that premarital sex was against my faith. I don't think he ever believed me. You see, in Iraq, Muslim men see Christian girls as loose and promiscuous. I could see Muhammad viewed me in the same manner. So, I broke up with him."

"Wait a second," I interrupted, "did I hear you accurately? Did you state that Muslim men view Christian women as promiscuous?"

"Yeh, definitely. For one thing, we dress as Western women do, and Muslim men see this as a sign of promiscuity."

"Certainly, this does not apply to ALL Muslim men? I

mean, there are moderate Muslim men who are open minded and tolerant of Christianity?"

"You haven't lived in Iraq."

"No, I haven't, but I think it's important to avoid generalizations."

Nadia simply shot me a skeptical look, as if to say, "You're naïve." Then, she continued her story.

Anyway, Muhammad recognized me. I was curious as to why he and other inmates were being detained. So, I asked one of the contractors, Mahmood, "Why are these men in prison?"

Mahmood answered, "they planted IED's to kill American and Iraqi Security Forces."

I would later research the meaning of the acronym, IED because, in all honesty, I was embarrassed I didn't know its meaning. I learned IED stands for Improvised Explosive Devices. Perhaps Nadia was correct: perhaps I was indeed naïve.

"After Mahmood told me why the inmates were incarcerated, I was shocked, and to be honest, I thought I was in over my head. I mean I wanted a career, but this information really frightened me. Nonetheless, I persevered and continued to work. Work was important to me. I mean, why else did I go to university if not to work in my profession?"

"I understand", I replied.

"Anyway, in October 2004 I received an anonymous telephone call on my cell phone. It really scared me. The caller swore at me and demanded I stop working with the Americans or he and the resistance forces would rape and then kill me, and my family. I felt sick to my stomach when I heard this. I dropped my phone and threw up. I thought about quitting my job, but I was stubborn and I wanted to work. I threw away the cell phone, as if by so doing, I had eliminated the threat."

"I was wrong."

"I went home and told my father."

"My dad asked, 'What did the caller say, word for word?'"

"I replied, 'He said, "You're a dirty Christian infidel, a whore and a traitor to our people!"'"

"My dad was very worried. You see, he knew that individuals who worked for the Americans were being killed by insurgents and terrorists. He believed in the American efforts to bring democracy to Iraq, but he was terrified of the opposition. He was terrified for me, for my safety. My dad and I discussed this call a lot. He felt that Muhammad had informed other insurgents that I was working for the Americans. What my father didn't know is that I had actually dated him. He would not have approved. You see, in Iraq, it's difficult for Muslims and Christians to marry. A Christian woman would have to convert, but a Muslim man would not. Anyway, I know Muhammad's real motivation in telling the insurgents about me was his sense of rejection when I ended our relationship, when I wouldn't sleep with him."

"Nadia, tell me about your relationship with Muhammad."

"Well, in the beginning he was charming. He was kind and supportive. He seemed to love me for whom I was. He didn't want to change me. But then over time, when things got serious, he wanted to change me, to control me, and I didn't like it. I remember one day we went shopping at an outdoor market. He put on airs that he was being generous because he bought me a bunch of new clothes, but they were clothes I would never wear: long potato sack dresses down to my ankles, with long, loose sleeves. I told him they weren't my taste. He said, "Haram, you reflect on me now, so don't be a whore. Wear them.'"

I shot back right at him and said, "I'm not Muslim. I'm not wearing these potato sacks.'"

"Muhammad became red in the face, and then he spit at me, as one would at a dog, not even a dog. Then he shouted, 'Act like a woman. Stop shouting. It's not feminine. Behave!'" So, I began to listen to him because I thought I was being promiscuous if I didn't. I wore the clothes he bought me. I had no choice. He had burned all of my Westernized clothes, anyway."

"Wow", I interjected. "Muhammad really manipulated you. I mean, what better way to control a woman, particularly a Christian woman, than to question her sexual mores and morals?"

"Exactly, but then, it got worse over time. He brought me to a mosque in Baghdad. I was forced to wear the burka and sit with the women behind the men. An imam was lecturing about politics and I raised my hand to ask a question. The mosque became silent. No one talked or moved. Then the imam said to Muhammad, 'Control your woman.' An elderly Muslim woman took me away to the kitchen to prepare lunch and I thought, 'I guess I know where my place is here in this mosque.' That was the end of the relationship for me. There was no way I was going to waste my education to end up cooking and cleaning in a kitchen, whether it is at home or in a mosque."

"Good girl!" I exclaimed. I couldn't help myself. I tried to remain unemotional as a lawyer, but as a woman, I was offended by the chauvinism displayed at this mosque, and I was exuberant Nadia had rebelled. I felt as if she took a stand for ALL women.

"Thanks", laughed Nadia, you do understand, don't you?"

"Absolutely, and I think it took a great deal of moral strength for you to stand up against the imam and Muhammad."

Nadia smiled radiantly. I could discern the seeds of Rejuvenation, of Rebirth, of Spring Time, transfixing and transfiguring her face. Finally, I could see some color.

She continued her story, but with more sap in her voice.

"Well, in late October 2004 I was driving in my car when another car pulled up and cut me off. A man came out of the car. He was dressed all in black and wore a ski mask sort of thing. He terrified me. He shot at my car with an AK-47 gun. Thank God I was able to escape unharmed but I was really shaken up. I remember my legs felt like water. I don't even remember how I drove home that day. But, when I arrived, my dad was outside and he said, 'What happened to you?' It was then that I noticed two or three bullet holes in my car.

'Are you alright?' my dad asked.

'Yeh, yeh, don't worry', I replied, but my dad was worried. He said, 'Listen, you need to stop working for that company, or at least talk to your boss. Tell him what happened. Ask him for protection.'

'O.K. I'll talk to my boss.'

"I was angry Muhammad would cause me so much damage just because I didn't want him, just because I wouldn't sleep with him, like the Christian infidel he thought I was. I was stubborn. I was idealistic. I was stupid."

"No, you were far from unintelligent. I'm outraged at what Muhammad did to you."

"So, I went to work later that day and told my boss what happened. I was surprised and disappointed in his reaction. It was as if he didn't care about my safety. I was no longer useful to him, and so, he could simply dispose of me. He said, 'Well, there's not much I can do for you. I mean maybe you should just take some vacation time.'

I responded, 'I don't need vacation time. I need protection.'"

He said bluntly, 'Well, you knew what you were getting into when I hired you, so what do you want from me now?'

'Nothing', was all I said. Then, I turned around and left for good."

"Did you go to the police and report this crime?" I asked.

"No, I didn't go to the police because I was afraid to tell them I worked for the Americans."

"But the police are there to protect you as an Iraqi citizen, and they should remain objective, yes?

"No, the insurgents and the terrorists have infiltrated the police and so, the police can't be trusted."

"Are you suggesting there are no trustworthy police officers, officers who are genuine in their mandate to protect the public?"

"No, there are, but the police officers who are not corrupt are powerless against the terrorists and the insurgents. They have families too, you know. Their families are threatened all the time. So, there is nothing they can do to help Iraqis. They're human. They don't want to risk the lives of their wives, children, brothers and sisters, you know."

"Anyway, after talking to my boss, I didn't go home. It

wasn't safe. Instead, I went to my aunt's house. I went into hiding for weeks. It wasn't easy. I kept having nightmares about the shooting and the man in black. I couldn't talk to my aunt because no one really wants to hear such things. It scares them. Over time, I grew restless. I was used to working. Staying in hiding was driving me crazy. I kept busy reading and studying. I helped my aunt at home, with domestic things, but to be honest, all she did was cook and clean for her eight children. I wasn't used to this, and it bored me to death. So, one day, I decided to go for a walk, to get some air. I thought it was no big deal, just a walk."

"I was about to leave my aunt and uncle's home, when she stopped me, and said, 'You need to wear the burka for your own protection. It's not safe. All the women in our neighborhood are wearing it now when they go out.'"

"This hit a sensitive spot with me and so I said, 'I'm not Muslim, so why should I be forced to wear the burka?'"

'Do you want to be kidnapped, killed, or worse, raped?'

'No, of course not.'

'So, please wear this burka. It'll fit you.'

'So, I wore the black burka and alighted outside. I looked at my cousin's bicycle, the one he rode every single day, so freely, without a second thought. But, the image of me on a bicycle, with a flying burka stopped me. I knew better. I had never seen a Muslim woman on a bicycle before in my entire life.'

'Let me clarify: Christian girls and women were forced to wear the burka, a symbol of Islam. Otherwise, they would run the risk of sexual assault, rape, or murder?'

'Yeh, at that time Christian girls were kidnapped, raped, forced to marry Muslim men and even killed. So, it was wise to wear the burka for our own safety and protection. You know, our faith would not protect us. The burka would.'

'How ironic and manipulative of radical Muslims', was all I said out loud, but my mind was a whirl. I made a mental note to research the issue of religious freedom in Iraq. I required objective corroboration for Nadia's future refugee claim before the Immigration and Refugee Board in Toronto, Ontario. Sure enough, according to the International Religious Freedom Report 2008, Released by the Bureau of Democracy, Human Rights, and Labor,

> 95% of the population is Muslim and only 5% is Christian. Women and girls were often threatened for refusing to wear the hijab, for dressing in Western-style clothing, or for failing to adhere sufficiently to strict interpretations of conservative Islamic norms governing public behavior. Numerous women, including Christians, reported opting to wear the hijab for security purposes after being harassed for not doing so. On December 10, 2007 police in the southern city of Basrah discovered the bullet ridden bodies of Christian Maisoon Marzouq and her brother, Osama. According to the Basrah police, the case was one of 40 during 2007, where women, regardless of religion, were murdered for not covering their heads and conforming to a conservative Muslim style of dress.

Unfortunately, history is repeating itself. At the present time, ISIS has infiltrated Iraq and they are abducting Christian girls and women. Girls and women of the Yezidi minority are subjected to sexual violence, rape and torture. Hundreds and possibly thousands of young girls and women are forcibly married, sold as chattel and given as *gifts* to ISIS fighters and supporters. Many of these girls and women are forced to convert to Islam. Rape is utilized as a weapon, a violent instrument with which to commit war crimes and crimes against humanity.

Reading about persecution and actually meeting and listening to a victim face to face, are two entirely different things. As I sat listening to Nadia's story, I was deeply moved as much as I was profoundly outraged. I took that anger and channeled it into winning Nadia's refugee claim. I felt compelled to. Nadia was much more than just a case for me: she was a human being who had suffered degrading atrocities simply because she is Christian; she is a woman; and she worked.

"Please continue, Nadia", I pierced through the air of dense emotional pain and anguish. The pain was palpable, and, frankly, it made me sick, quite literally sick to my stomach. I would question any human being who would not feel ill after listening to Nadia's story. Just listening to her story was taking a toll on me. However, I drew solace in my belief that I had already heard the worst parts.

I was wrong.

"Well, I walked for two hours. It was good to get out into the fresh air. I felt so much better after the walk. But, someone must have seen me because late at night at 3 a.m. we were all wakened up by pounding at the door. My cousin, Yousef answered in his pyjamas. He was met by six insurgents who barged in. One of them took the butt of his gun and rammed it into my cousin's skull. He fell unconscious to the ground. My aunt screamed. She was hysterical. I'll never forget her screams. All of us ran downstairs. It was then that I saw Muhammad. I had never seen such hatred in his eyes before. I didn't recognize him anymore. Maybe I just never knew him.

It was hard to believe that once we actually loved each other. He gave me a cold, hard, vicious stare, and then he said, 'I'll take this one.'"

"I was paralyzed. I couldn't move." 'Please, please,' was all I could say to him. But he never heard me. He had one thing on his mind, and one thing only. He said, 'You f --- whore. You wouldn't let me have you back then, eh? Well, now I'm going to take you. Are you a virgin? I doubt it, you Christian whore, infidel. How many men have you been with? What about those Americans you work for? How many of them have you slept with? You American whore! Why do you think they wanted you? For your translation skills?' He laughed. It was an evil, frightening laugh. It was terrifying."

'Muhammad, for the love of God, please. I've done nothing to you. Why are you doing this?'

'Because you're a whore for the Americans, that's why, a shamarta.'

"The stench of Muhammad made me vomit. He wasn't hygienic. He breathe had a rotten teeth stench. He had never taken care of his teeth. They were black and rotten. He was a chain smoker and his breathe smelled like wet, rotten cigarettes. He put his mouth on mine, more like he was swallowing me than kissing me. Then, he started to bite me. It really hurt. My mouth began to bleed. He pulled my hair back hard, and screamed at me, 'See if you covered like I told you to, this wouldn't be happening to you now, would it?' I never knew a person could hate another person so much. He cut off my underwear with a knife, and then he raped me. I was a virgin. It hurt. It really, really hurt. He laughed when he discovered I was a virgin."

"He said, 'Surprise. Surprise. You were saving yourself for

me, right? Good girl. So, then, you get to live. Otherwise, I would have had to kill you. Like this –' Then, he grabbed my aunt by her hair, and shot her in the head, execution style. I can still taste her blood. It splashed all over my face. 'See how lucky you are', he said.

"That same night, Muhammad abducted me and took me to his home. He said we were going to get married now. I was in shock. He didn't care. He raped me over and over again that night. This time, I didn't care. In the morning, Muhammad's sister, Noor told me Muhammad wanted me to wear the burka now. She gave me one of hers to wear. I did. Then, Muhammad took me out shopping for more burkas. But, he also bought the most vulgar, disgusting and degrading lingerie for me to wear. He said, 'You wear this for me.' It wasn't my taste, but he didn't care. I had to be covered in public, but in private, I had to dress like a prostitute for his pleasure."

"He had sex with me whenever he felt like it. He said, 'You have to make yourself available for me whenever I want, understand?' In the beginning, I knew what he was doing was wrong, but then, over time, it began to feel normal. I just gave in to him. Now, I'm so ashamed. I think I even started to fall in love with him."

"Nadia," I felt compelled to interject, "Are you certain you fell in love with him? I mean, love is a choice. What choice did you have? He abducted you. You were not free to leave. Perhaps the feelings you think you had for him were a coping mechanism, a way to survive. You had to convince yourself you were in love with him to endure the tremendous trauma and the sheer horror of your experience."

"You're right. I didn't have a choice. Also, his sister was on his side, and she made me feel like I was crazy and not

Muhammad. Actually, truthfully, he made me sick. I used to drink wine before we had sex. I had to numb myself to have sex with him. He made me convert to Islam. I didn't want to. But, I had no choice. I just regurgitated what he told me to think and say, and then over time, I began to actually believe in Islam."

"That's a program of strategic and intense indoctrination. First, Muhammad rapes you; then he murders your aunt right in front of your eyes, and then he abducts you and continues to rape you repeatedly over an extended period of time. He broke your spirit so that you couldn't fight him. He forced you to convert to Islam, to wear the burka against your own wishes. Then, he forces you to wear lingerie with which you are uncomfortable, again, against your wishes. He denigrated and degraded you, Nadia."

"Yeh, he did. It was all so strange for me. In public, Muhammad wanted me to wear the burka. He was so strict about that. I had to look like a chaste, proper, good Muslim woman. But, in private, he forced me to do some horrible, degrading sexual things, things I would never ordinarily do. Like, he would have sex with me from behind. It really hurt."

"What do you mean, from behind?"

"You know, not the normal way, like from your behind."

I felt nauseated. Poor Nadia was so degraded and dehumanized by this man. I also did not understand the duplicity involved in forcing a woman to wear the burka in public, and then promiscuous lingerie in private. This duplicity was akin to the Madonna/Medusa complex: completely devoid of honesty and dignity. Isn't a woman who wears Western clothes both in public and private more honest than a woman who wears the ultra-conservative burka in public, and then vulgar lingerie in private? Shouldn't a woman be allowed to feel comfortable in her own attire, and by extension, in her own skin? I thought about the women in North America who wear colorful hijabs, heavy handed make-up and tight fitting clothing. It seemed to me they drew more attention to themselves than women who wore regular clothing.

Nadia pierced through my reverie. "Muhammad's favorite outfit was a red leather underwear and red leather tank top. It was something a woman would wear in a bordello. I hated it. He would become so aroused whenever he forced me to put this outfit on, which was far too often. I felt degraded. Then, he would have sex with me in a violent way."

Nadia broke down and sobbed. I let her. She needed to. Then, I spoke softly, "Nadia, what you describe is not making love; it is making hate. That's why you're so drained and empty. Love is supposed to nurture and nourish you. You should feel strong through love. Muhammad abused you in every sense, physically, psychologically, emotionally and spiritually. I'm amazed you're here telling me your story."

"You're right. I never thought about Muhammad in this way. He never made love with me. He made hate with me. In Iraq at that time, many Christian women were raped. It was a weapon of war."

"Well put, Nadia. You're absolutely correct. Unfortunately, throughout history men have utilized sexual assault and rape as a weapon of war, as a weapon of mass destruction."

"But, I agreed to sex. That's what makes me feel so ashamed."

"No, Nadia, you didn't consent to sex. You had no choice. What would have happened to you if you didn't give in to Muhammad?"

"He would have beaten me and then killed me, just as he murdered my aunt, without a thought, without remorse. After he killed her, he actually ate a full meal. I couldn't believe he had an appetite. One time, I didn't feel well enough to have sex with him and I told him as much. He didn't even hear me. He went ahead anyway. But, he never listened to me. He never heard me. So, over time, I felt invisible. Over time, I stopped listening and hearing myself."

"That's the ultimate form of control: when the abuse and neglect is internalized, a woman is truly lost to herself. I've seen this far too often."

"Why do I feel so ashamed? I mean, I've dishonored my family. My sister, Zeina was lucky she was killed. I wish I had been killed too. It would have been better than this."

"Nadia, how precisely have you dishonored your family? You are the victim here, not the culprit."

"But, my family is ashamed of me. They feel I've brought shame to them by being raped."

"Then, your family has dishonored you, and not the other way around."

"I can't sleep. I eat too much. Actually, I can't stop eating. I've put on fifty pounds."

"Often victims of sexual assault or rape put on weight as a protective mechanism. They believe that if they put on weight, and become unattractive, men will not look at them, and therefore will not rape them. It's as if the extra weight is like a safety blanket. But, when a woman is unhappy with the extra weight, then it is akin to the burka, correct, a form of imprisonment, of repression and suppression. To my mind, you should seek counseling. You need to speak to a qualified psychiatrist or social worker about the horrifying and horrific experience you endured. If you don't it will eat at you and over time, it will consume and destroy you."

"I thought the hell I lived with Muhammad was the worst thing of all, but it's not. It's surviving which is far, far worse."

"No, Nadia. Surviving is a tribute to the strength of your spirit, your character. You are allowing Muhammad to win by viewing your survival as a form of punishment, aren't you? I mean, he's inside your head. Get him out. Again, I cannot stress to you the importance of counseling."

"I can' talk about Muhammad. It only makes it worse. I can't relive this anymore."

"I understand, but aren't you reliving the trauma by not venting? Counseling will afford you the opportunity to rid yourself of this toxic energy, to rid yourself of Muhammad and what he has done to you and to your family."

"One day, I found out I was pregnant and the thought of bringing his child into this world was overwhelming for me. I didn't want his baby. So, I threw myself down a flight of stairs. I miscarried later on that night. Abortions go against my Christian faith. I killed my own child, a life. I can't live with this guilt."

"At the time, you weren't thinking clearly. You were in the middle of hell. If you had been pregnant by a man you genuinely loved, would you have made the same choice?"

"No, of course not. But, I can't have children anymore. After I threw myself down the stairs, I spent the night in the bathroom on the toilet. I kept hemorrhaging all night long. There were big clots of blood. I didn't dare say anything to Muhammad. He thought I was having my period. So now, I'm sterile. I did it to myself. But, I knew that having a baby with Muhammad would have sealed my fate with him forever. There is no way he would have let me go after having his child. I always hoped I would be free of him."

"Nadia, stop blaming yourself. Put the blame squarely on Muhammad's shoulders. That's where it belongs. He damaged you. He almost destroyed you."

"What man will want me now?"

"What about yourself? Do you want yourself? Isn't that more important?"

"What do you mean?"

"How can you expect some man to love you when you don't love yourself? You need to learn to take care of yourself. Cherish yourself. Respect yourself. Do what makes you, Nadia, happy. Do the things in life which bring you joy and peace – whatever they may be."

"But, I hate myself. Look at how fat I've become. I used to be slim. But I kept over eating when I was with Muhammad. Actually, he liked me fat. He said so. He used to say, don't lose weight. I like a big bum and big breasts."

"That's repulsive. You're a sexual being, Nadia, not a sexual object. What about what you like? What about your own self-image. How do you want to look, Nadia?"

"Well, I like myself slim, like I used to be. I used to enjoy riding a bicycle. But, Muhammad told me it's haram – you know, shameful. In fact, Muhammad thought it was somehow promiscuous for a woman to exercise. In Iraq, many Muslim men feel this way. I have never seen a Muslim woman on a bicycle, you know? So, now, I just eat and smoke. I can't stop. I feel sick all the time. I can't breathe even. I can't exercise because I smoke. So, I eat more. Then I smoke more."

"It's a vicious circle. Nadia, many abused women overeat, smoke, take illicit drugs, engage in unhealthy relationships and the like. They essentially internalize their abuse. The best defense against this internalization is learning to love yourself."

"You're right. I'm involved with a man right now and I'm not happy. His name is Naseer. He's a Muslim from Lebanon. I'm so confused. If he tells me to just sit there and wait for him, I do. It's as if I can't move. I hate myself for this weakness. I can see he's controlling and manipulating me, but I can't say anything. "

"What do you mean? Give me an example."

"Well, if he pressures me to do something I'm uncomfortable with, I just do it, all the while knowing I'm not comfortable with it. Things like wearing the clothes he wants me to wear, like the burka."

"Are you wearing the burka by choice? If it's your choice, that's one thing, but if it's by force, that's an entirely different matter."

"No, I hate this burka. He wants me to wear it, not me. But, I don't know how to say, 'No.'"

"Just say it. It's that simple. Nadia, I have represented abused women for over ten years. These men who abuse are really, truly cowards deep down inside. They present as bullies, but bullies are thinly veiled cowards."

"Nasser is just another Muhammad, you know."

"Exactly. Victims of abuse commonly repeat the same pattern with different men. You've been conditioned to relinquish your own will to that of Muhammad. It's as if he erased your own sense of autonomy. So, over time when someone keeps chiseling away at your autonomy, you forget to exercise it. However, and this is a critical caveat – retrieving your autonomy is like riding a bicycle for the very first time after years of not doing so: once you get back on that bicycle, you'll remember how to ride it, and you'll be free."

"I don't even know how to begin."

"You begin by listening to yourself. Listen to that voice within you. It's your moral compass. For instance, if you feel uncomfortable wearing the burka, then take it off. It's that simple. If you are uncomfortable around Nasser, then end the relationship. My father used to give me advice about men. He would say, "Just sit quietly with a man and truly listen to the way you feel. If you feel uncomfortable, run – and run fast without looking back."

Nadia looked perplexed and confused. So, I asked her one simple question, "How do you feel when you're around Naseer?"

"Very uncomfortable."

"How long have you been seeing him?"

"About six months."

"Yet, despite your feelings of discomfort, inspired by the very person with whom you're supposed to feel the *most* comfortable, you remain in the relationship?"

"Weird, right?"

"No, it's not weird, it's common among victims of abuse. But, know this: a man who genuinely loves you accepts and cherishes you just as you are, not in his own image, but as you are."

"That's not Nasser. He isn't good for me."

"Good, that's a beginning."

"Now, what do I do? I mean, it's confusing for me. I don't know who I am, what I want from life. I'm so used to men defining me."

"Well, I have a suggestion: if you want, take off that

burka, go for a bicycle ride and feel the wind on your face and in your hair."

However, Nadia was not ready for that bicycle ride yet. She continued her story.

"After six months of the abduction, my father just showed up at my door. I was shocked by his appearance. He had aged. He told me the man who had raped and killed my sister, Zeina, was Muhammad's cousin. My dad also said our family was fleeing Iraq to Syria, and I had to come. This is how I escaped Muhammad. We fled to Syria during the night. Once there, we contacted my mother's cousin in Windsor, Ontario. We were smuggled into Canada for $10,000.00 euros each."

"I was struck by Nadia's statement regarding Muhammad's cousin. It led me to think that often an act may be viewed as a political or religious statement, when, it signifies a personal vendetta. People use religion to hide their true motivations, their own agenda. Radicalized individuals, whether Muslim, Christian or any faith, use and abuse religion to further their own interests. They distort religion to reflect their own image, rather than to reflect the image of God."

Nadia's hearing before the Immigration and Refugee Board was held after a two year wait. This protracted delay took its toll on her. She desperately needed a sense of stability. She could not fully heal until she had that sense that she had finally found a safe haven, that she would not be deported to Iraq, the stage of her persecution.

Unfortunately, Nadia was not a good witness at the hearing. Her psychiatrist had put her on anti-anxiety medication, which led to her mind wandering all over the place. At one point in the hearing, I advised her, "Nadia, keep your eye on the ball", to which she responded, "What ball?" Even the Panel Member had to laugh.

At the conclusion of the hearing, the Panel Member reserved her decision. But, two months later, we received the judge's ruling. We won Nadia's refugee claim. Of course, my assistant and I were extremely happy and excited for Nadia. She could finally breathe. My assistant called Nadia immediately, and just as quickly Nadia attended my office. She was ecstatic when I informed her that the decision was positive. She left my office, but returned shortly thereafter with a token of her appreciation: a dozen white roses, my favorite.

I gave her a bicycle....

Just a Cup of Tea

SARA APPEARED TO be in her late 50's, although later I learned she was only 40 years of age. She was small of stature, emaciated, with a dark complexion overshadowed by a yellow tinge. She appeared as if she smoked a pack of cigarettes a day, of course, behind closed doors. You see, in her country, women were prohibited from smoking in public. Certainly, she was malnourished, both physically and emotionally. She appeared as if she weighed but 100 pounds – if that. I could discern that she was a beautiful woman in her youth, but her marital problems had devoured her spirit and left their mark on her face. I think smoking was a mechanism with which she coped with her husband, the Holy Imam.

I asked her, "How can I help you?" It was then that she relayed her story to me. It was clear that she desperately needed to articulate her ordeal out loud to another woman, although why she chose me was a mystery.

I'm married to an Imam, Mohammed in Saudi Arabia. I have four boys, ages 8 to 18. I didn't work in Saudi. I stayed home and raised my children. My husband was very controlling. I had to ask his permission to do anything in life, even to call or visit my own family. If I were to do anything "wrong" he would threaten me and tell me he would send me to the moral house for bad women. I believed him. He's an Imam.

One night, I was asleep in our bedroom when he woke me up and commanded me to leave the bed. He didn't even say "hello." I knew that I couldn't ask him any questions. I wasn't allowed to even talk to him when he first came home. That was one of his rules. So, I left our bed, our marital bed. Past experience taught me that asking him any questions, defying his authority in any manner would only result in a beating. I was too tired for a beating that night. It's not easy taking care of four boys, cooking, cleaning, you know – a woman's work.

Although I did not interrupt her at that point, I thought, "This poor woman is so defeated by the abuse, she doesn't even realize she's diminishing her own horrendous experience. My God, she actually said, she's too tired for a beating that night. She didn't say that beatings are wrong. Further, as a professional woman, I thought her comment about the definition of a woman's work was demeaning and extremely sad."

Nonetheless, there was something in her eyes, some drowning, but still flickering flame, which drew me in. I was riveted. I was determined to help this woman rekindle this flame before it was completely submerged in a sea of tears, in her silent soul of past and permanent tears.

She continued her story.

So, I walked half asleep into our kitchen to make myself a cup of tea. All I wanted at that point was to drink my tea in peace. An hour later, my husband entered the kitchen and demanded that I have sex with him. I'm sorry. Forgive me for using that word, but that's what he wanted. He approached me. He smelled like another woman, and so I asked, "What's going on?" He replied calmly as if nothing was wrong, "I married another woman tonight. She's in the bedroom. You have my permission to change one of the spare rooms into your own bedroom, but don't spend too much money on it. Hiba is a new bride, and I have to buy her nice things."

I felt as if he had kicked me in the stomach. I couldn't breathe. I started to cry. He didn't even try to console me. He was ice. Eventually, I asked him, "How old is she?" He was proud of himself when he stated she was only 16 years old. My husband is 59 years old. "She's younger than our own son", I admonished.

That was my first mistake.

He responded, "Listen, I'm your husband and you have certain wifely duties toward me. You know a man has needs, and you're supposed to be available for me whenever I want. So, do it." I recoiled. There was no way I was going to have sex with him when he just finished with a 16 year old girl in our own bedroom. She was still there. So, he kicked me and shouted at me, "Listen, you're like a ball. When I kick you against the wall, you'll just bounce back to me." That's when I vomited. I received a bad beating that night….. His new child bride remained in our bedroom. Perhaps she was frightened by my cries as her new father/husband was beating me. Perhaps she was afraid she was next. After all, she was only 16. I fell asleep that night, actually feeling sorry for her.

That was my second mistake.

The next morning, she awoke and danced her way into the kitchen. She demanded I make her coffee. I responded, "Make it yourself." She replied, "I'm telling Mohammed." I could not believe it. Here she was a child of 16, younger than my own son, and she was ordering me around - so much for feeling sorry for her. I didn't make her coffee. She did without because she didn't know how to make it. I guess she didn't need to know how to make coffee or cook. She was his toy wife.

That day was one of the longest days of my life. She treated my children badly. It was clear she wanted nothing to do with them. In turn, my children wanted nothing to do with her. She lounged around all day, like a lazy cat, watching television, reading beauty magazines, exercising, putting on make-up, dying her long black hair, first red, then blond, painting her long fingernails, then her toe nails – all in preparation for my husband's bed. I thought, O.K. I understand. She views me as the Servant Wife. As a Muslim woman, I knew her view of me came from my husband. You see, Muslim women think whatever their husbands tell them to think.

I couldn't stand it. I thought I was going to have a nervous breakdown. to I called my father. Immediately, he came over. You see, I was one of the lucky ones in Saudi because my father understood how much pain I was in, and he didn't beat or cheat on my mother. So, I vented, cried and he listened. In the end, he said, "O.K. Don't worry. Leave it in my hands. I'll talk to Mohammed. This isn't right." Before he left, he gave me a big hug and I felt safe in his arms like I did when I was just a little girl. He's a good father.

My father did speak to my husband. He tried to convince Mohammed about how wrong it was to marry another woman and bring her in our home, in our bedroom. My husband responded, "I can't afford two houses, one for Sara and one for my new bride, Hiba". My father responded, "My daughter's highly educated. She's not Hiba's servant. My husband yelled at him and said, "If you want your daughter so badly, take her.

I'll keep the boys and Hiba. Take her tonight. She's yours. I don't want the responsibility. It's cheaper for me if you take her back. She's your daughter. She's your responsibility now, not mine."

So, that night, my father took me into his home, where I remained for two weeks. However, I missed my children. My father called my husband and asked for his permission to visit our children. I went to see our children as soon as my husband granted his permission. Our boys were miserable. Hiba didn't cook or clean for them. The house was filthy. Their grades went down. My youngest son, Hassan, cried and cried. He begged me to come home. He said, "Mama, I miss you. I don't like Hiba. She's mean to us. When we tell dad, he says, she's just a girl. She misses her home. Be good to her. Treat her like your own sister." When I heard those words, I felt like vomiting. My children were supposed to treat their father's 16 year old second wife like a sister?

"Yes," I interceded, "that's really twisted."

Sara just looked at me with this vacuous expression in her eyes. I was fearful her flame would be extinguished. So, I reassured her, "Sara, I'm sorry you had to go through such tremendous abuse." I gave her a hug. She continued her story.

Thank you for saying that about Hiba. You see, with Muslims, sisters are holy, and so when a man says, "you're like my sister" he means, I can't touch you. For my husband to tell our boys to think of Hiba like a sister is really sick. He should have thought of Hiba like a daughter. Anyway, what was I supposed to do? Obviously, Hiba hated me and my children. How could I leave them alone with her? Mohammed didn't seem to care, as long as he was having sex with Hiba, that's all that mattered to him. Hiba seemed perfectly content with

Mohammed. I didn't understand both of them. They both made me sick. But, I really had no choice. I returned home to my children.

That was my third mistake.

That's when things got really bad. Hiba hated me. She expected me to be her servant. I took care of my children, cooked and cleaned, but there was no way I was going to take care of Hiba. Of course, she would use sex to turn Mohammed against me. She poisoned his mind. She wasn't as innocent as she appeared to be. It was obvious to me that she knew a lot about sex and how to please a man. I wondered where she learned all this stuff.

"Holy shit!" I exclaimed. "Oh, sorry, Sara, that just came out."

Sara laughed. "You're funny," she stated. "Are you sure you're married to an Arab?"

"Yes, but why do you ask that?"

"Arab men kill their women's sense of humor."

"Sara, you know you're dead inside when you can't laugh anymore."

"Well, many Arabic women, especially Muslim women, don't laugh. Anyway, Mohammed began to beat me every single night. Before Hiba, the beatings were just three or four times a week. It was all her fault."

I felt compelled to interrupt her. I asked her, "Do you realize what you just said? You said that before your husband would beat you only three or four times a week. That's not the point. One beating is unacceptable. Plus, don't you think that your husband is responsible for the beatings, and not Hiba? She's only 16. Isn't she just as much a victim as you were?"

She just stared at me for a long time and then she asked, "Alex, excuse me, but are you sure you're married to an Arab?"

In typical lawyer fashion, I thought, "How is this relevant?" However, I didn't articulate this question because Sara didn't need lawyer ease at this point – she needed emotional support.

Yes, Sara, my husband is Arabic, but why do you ask?

"Well, then you should know that Arab men beat their wives."

"No, I don't know that," I said, "not all Arabic men beat their wives."

Again, she gave me a puzzled look punctuated by a pregnant pause, "But, that's why I came to you because you understand the Arabic culture and Islam."

"Well, there are times, Sara, when Arabic culture and Islam are all Greek to me."

"I thought you're Italian."

"No, no, Sara: 'It's all Greek to me' is an idiom."

"Don't say that. You're not an idiot."

I couldn't help but burst out laughing. Sara just stared at me in her polite, repressive manner. So, I attempted to clarify for her, "Sara an idiom is a cliché, an expression."

Again, she just stared at me in confusion. But, then, she seemed to absorb the clarification, and she too burst out laughing. She had a beautiful, wholesome, laughter, a laugher which highlighted her latent and natural beauty.

"O.K, " I responded, "so now, we're on the same page."

Again – that blank look of utter confusion. So, from that point on, I vowed to avoid clichés and idioms.

"O.K. Sara, we're getting off track. I just want to be clear. Surely, you don't believe all Arabic men, whether Muslim or

Christian, beat their wives? Domestic violence crosses lines of ethnicity, nationality, religion, culture, education and financial status. Sara, there is domestic abuse even here in Canada."

Her response was, "You've never lived in Saudi."

"No, I haven't."

We stared at each other deeply. I could feel her pain. It was palpable. I spoke softly against the tumultuous thunder of my sense of moral outrage. How could a man treat his wife, the mother of his children in this way? How could he turn her children against her? I thought Muslim men respected mothers. Isn't motherhood holy in Islam? How could the Saudi society tolerate such abuse against women? How could this society allow him to marry a child? Is this even legal there? Where are Hiba's parents in all of this? And who is Hiba? Is she a victim as I would believe? Or, is she calculating and shrewd as Sara believes? I had no frame of reference with which to answer any of my questions. I was totally confused and totally riveted. Sara could sense my confusion.

"Alex, in our culture and religion, women are as much our enemies as men. We don't stick together. We turn on each other. What do you think? Do you think that just because a girl wears the hijab, she's innocent? No, she's not. Many girls and women who wear the hijab are the first ones to really hurt another woman, to break up families."

"Wow. I guess I'm viewing your world from a Canadian angle. I see the hijab and I think, she must be so chaste and innocent."

"No, our women, our covered women, are not as good as you believe. They turn on each other like cats when it comes to who gets the man, who gets the financial support. They will use any weapon they have, especially sex."

"So, what you're saying is that there is no female solidarity."

Again, she gave me a look of confusion.

"I mean, women don't stick together."

"Yes, I already told you that."

I just laughed. In turn, she gave me this look which bespoke the words, "weren't you listening?" However, I was happy she gave me this look of annoyance because it meant her flame was springing back to life. She was annoyed, and it was great that she felt comfortable enough with me to express that genuine feeling. Based on what she had conveyed to me thus far, she had not been permitted to express herself in her country, in her home. She had been suppressed. She had buried her true feelings for so long that she had become ill, and that's precisely what happens to abused women. They internalize the abuse. They internalize the anger. The men who abuse them won't allow them to express their anger, pain, suffering, outrage, and so they bury all this pain inside their bodies, which in turn, inevitably, makes them physically, emotionally and psychologically ill. But, poor women, what choice do they have? It's not safe for them to express their anger at the very men who are hurting them.

I didn't need to articulate any of this to Sara. She could sense I understood. We had a connection, a connection based on empathy, compassion and humanity. You don't need to speak the same language for that sort of thing. You don't even need to speak any words. You just need to feel.

"You understand me."

"Yes. O.K. Sara, please continue with your story."

So, she did so.

"Things got worse and worse at home. My health started to go down. I would go to the doctor and he would say,

'O.K. just go home and be a good wife. What's your problem anyway? He would prescribe pills, sedatives and anti- depressants. I mean so many women in Saudi live on pills and smoke secretively, but I couldn't go on living this way. I couldn't be a good mother if I was drugged up all the time. I couldn't be a good mother when I was sick all the time. But, what could I do? The men have all the power in my country. So, I just tried to stay out of Mohammed's way, and focused on my children, like a good Muslim Mother."

"Sara," I said, "being a good Muslim mother doesn't mean you have to tolerate abuse. It's not good to tolerate abuse. Being good means you take care of yourself as well as your children. Don't you see?"

"I told you, you're not Muslim."

"O.K. I'm not Muslim, but I am a woman and a mother. So, I just want you to understand. I mean, you're in Canada, now, right? You can get some help with all this brainwashing nonsense. You should get some counseling. I think it would help you to begin the process of de-programming, of healing. I can recommend some great women's groups which would help you to this end."

"O.K. I guess so, but isn't it shameful for me to talk bad about my husband?"

"No, it's not. What's shameful is the manner in which he treated you. Don't allow him to put the onus on you. It's his fault, not yours. You did nothing wrong. He did. You need to start thinking differently, more honestly, less like a victim. He brainwashed you. He abused you and then told you it's shameful for you to even talk about it. Of course he would say that. That protects him. That serves his best interests, doesn't it? So, don't allow him to continue to control you now when you're finally free of him. Don't allow him to control your thinking. Change it. He can't stop you now, can he?"

"I'm not that strong."

"Not now, but you will be. It takes time, Sara. It's a journey, and the first step is to break the silence. The silence only serves to reinforce the shame. It's like wearing a burka of shame."

"You think I shouldn't wear the hijab?"

"That's your choice, Sara. I mean, there's freedom of religion in the Charter, and so, if you want to wear the hijab, then wear it, but only wear it if you want to, Sara, not because you're forced to. Do you understand?"

That's when I was taken aback and rather surprised. Sara took off her hijab. I just looked at her and smiled.

"You know, Alex, in Saudi, when a girl or woman converts to Islam and begins to wear the hijab, all our women clap. They don't really mean it. They're not really happy. But, still they clap."

"It's like they're being welcomed into some sort of cult, right? The women clap, but it's not a genuinely joyful and natural clap. I get it – totally."

"Yeh."

"O.K. So what happened next at home?"

Sara sighed. It was a long sigh, a sigh which belied years and years of silent abuse. Then she continued with her story.

"The fighting at home was awful. The boys and Hiba fought constantly. Hiba would complain to my husband, and he in turn, would beat me. So, then, my husband started to brainwash our boys. He told them, 'Your mother is a bad woman. Don't listen to her. She doesn't know how to cook or take care of a husband. That's why we need Hiba. She knows how to treat a man.' Over time, my own sons turned on me.

At this point, Sara crumpled and cried. I let her cry for a long time. Clearly, she needed to rid herself of these emotional toxins. I felt so sorry for her. I tried hard not to cry myself, but I couldn't help it. Just listening to her was painful for me. I'm a woman and a mother. I too have boys. I was irate that her husband would turn the children against their own mother. I mean, if a boy hates his mother, clearly, he's going to hate his future wife. Isn't this the soil in which to breed misogyny? Just get a boy to hate his mother and he will hate all women. It's that simple. It's not as if these misogynistic men are that bright. On the contrary, they're quite primitive.

Sara tried valiantly to pull herself together. My heart went out to her. In time, she was able to carry on with her story. I admired her strength and courage.

"So, I didn't have a choice. If I stayed at home, I knew I would get very sick. What good would I be then to my children? I became very depressed. I couldn't even distract myself by going out because I needed my husband's permission to go out, and I couldn't go out without a male relative. You know, that's the way it is in Saudi."

"Hang on. Are you saying that all women cannot go out in Saudi Arabia unless they are accompanied by a male relative?"

Again, she gave me this look like, "Are you brain dead?"

"Well, of course, you should know. You're married to one."

I responded, "My God, you are completely brainwashed. You actually believe it's perfectly normal that a woman cannot leave her home unless first, she has the permission of her husband, and second, she is accompanied by a male relative."

Sara answered, "Are you sure you're married to an Arab?' to which I responded,

"Sara, again, not all Arab men are like your husband. In addition, in Canada, you can go outside without a male relative."

"I know, but it's not easy for me to go out alone even here in Canada."

"I know what you mean. It's like a bird in a cage. Once you open the door and let that bird free, the bird may be too frightened to fly away, right?"

"Exactly. I have a hard time leaving my apartment. I only go out to get food. But, I can only go as far as the corner store. I'm too afraid to go any further without a man relative, you know?"

As a woman, and as a lawyer, I was repulsed by such laws which prohibit a woman from free mobility rights.

So, I asked her, "Why do you think Saudi has such laws?"

She responded, "Well, they say it's for our own protection, so that we don't get raped, you know, but I think, it's just to control us."

Now, it was my turn to just stare at her in utter disbelief. This was my first time representing a victim of gender persecution from Saudi Arabia. I made a mental note: "Research women's rights and the laws pertaining to women in Saudi Arabia. Start with current United States Department of State Reports (DOS Reports) and the Immigration and Refugee Board Country Reports."

I proceeded to ask her, "Sara, do you know if women's mobility restrictions are a result of legislation or custom?"

"No, it's the law."

Still, I wanted to check this issue and ensure that Saudi

Arabia actually had laws which restricted a woman's mobility rights. Where were these laws? Were they in the Criminal Code? My mind was racing. I had so many questions. I needed objective evidence. I needed research.

"O.K., Sara, I'll check this point. What happened next?"

She replied, "Well, my father applied for a student visa for me. He thought I needed to get away. So, I got a student visa to study English. I left my boys. It was the hardest thing I ever had to do, but, I couldn't take it anymore. So, here I am now in Canada."

I just looked at her. Her story touched and moved me deeply. I asked her, "When you left Saudi did you intend on returning?"

"No", was all she said before she broke down again and cried.

Our interview lasted for over three hours. She had no money for this initial consultation. I didn't care. She touched my heart, and that was good enough for me. I really had no choice in this matter. I felt compelled to help her.

After she stopped crying I drove her to the train station. She was heading back to Toronto where she lived. She appeared frightened and fragile as she waved good-bye from her window. But, I could see that she was becoming stronger. She had not put that hijab back on. Rather, she was just wringing it with her fingers, a small act of defiance, a tremendous act of autonomy. You see, Sara had a choice to make: she could wear the hijab or not. She was fortunate enough that she could now make that choice of her own free will. No one would force her one way of the other. She chose not to wear the hijab. That spoke volumes about the authenticity of the hijab. If a woman freely chooses to wear it, that's fine, but if she has no choice, the hijab is not an authentic statement of a woman's true religious beliefs: it is a form of imprisonment.

Unfortunately, it took years for Sara to finally receive her hearing date before the Immigration and Refugee Board in Toronto. During these years, we kept in touch and developed a close relationship. I had connected Sara with Jewish Women's Charitable Groups which assisted her in acclimatizing to Canada. These groups assisted Sara in domestic matters, such as purchasing groceries, learning how to take a bus, open a bank account, compose a resume, find a job, and the like. Several members of one such group actually appeared with her at the hearing for moral support. These particular women had grown quite close to Sara and me. I had spoken with them a myriad of times over the telephone regarding Sara's adjustment to a completely foreign world, where she had to learn the most basic things, things she had never been able to do for herself in Saudi Arabia alone without her husband or a male relative. These were things North American women take for granted, for instance, we don't think twice about hopping into our cars and driving ourselves anywhere we wish or need to go. However, Sara had never in her life driven a car. She didn't know how to. She wasn't legally allowed to drive.

In any event, I was excited to finally represent Sara on the day of the refugee hearing. I was also excited to finally meet the women I had spoken to so often, but had never met face to face. One of them had called my office to inform me that they planned on being present at the hearing for moral support. We discussed Sara at length. We all felt she needed to feel safe. She needed to know she would not be deported back to Saudi Arabia where her abusive husband lived. She needed a safe haven, both geographically and emotionally. She was successful in receiving the later. She leaned on me emotionally, as she leaned on these women. However, Sara needed to become a Deemed Convention Refugee in order to truly feel safe. That was my job.

I had taken the early morning train at 6 a.m. for the afternoon hearing. It was a four hour ride to Toronto from Windsor. As I boarded Via Rail, I thought about the first time Sara had taken the same train for her initial consultation with me. She had changed exponentially – both inside and out. Sara went from being an apprehensive, chain-smoking, frightened, suppressed almost childlike woman to a more confident, happier, healthier, autonomous and stronger woman. She still had issues, emotional scars which would never heal. But, she was much happier.

All of us met just outside the hearings room. Sara appeared nervous and frightened. The women shrouded around her like a protective veil, only this time, there was no hypocrisy behind the protection. It was sincere. Of course, the women had a myriad of questions for me as Sara's lawyer. I expected this. I explained the process to them, and tried to assure them that everything was going to come out well. They thanked me for all I had done for Sara, and I, in turn, thanked them. Then one of the women stated, "Do your thing, and don't let us down." I know she meant well. However, her comment was somewhat nerve-wracking. I would do my best, but I just hoped it would be good enough as I didn't want to let Sara and all of her supporters down.

The panel member asked me for the names of the members of the Jewish Women's Charitable Organization, as well as their purpose for being present. I answered that their purpose was to offer moral support. They were not witnesses. The panel member simply nodded and officially commenced the hearing. Sara was sworn in. It was significant that she chose to make a Solemn Declaration rather than swear on the Koran or the Bible. She had changed. The panel member stated, "Counsel, I received your request for the reverse order of questioning, and I accept it. So, proceed." I had requested I be allowed to question Sara first, to illicit her testimony in a non-adversarial manner. I was elated the panel accepted my request.

Sara and I began our questioning as if she were simply telling her story to a friend or a sister, someone she trusted and with whom she felt comfortable. She testified about the abuse she had suffered at the hands of her husband, the physical and emotional abuse. It was heart wrenching. She spoke about the control he had over her, from simple decisions such as what to make for dinner to important decisions, such as birth control and how many children she wanted. At one point, she spoke about the number of abortions her husband forced her to have. This confused the panel member, and rightly so. So, she interceded,

"But, Mrs. F, please clarify for me. I don't understand. You're saying your husband forced you to have numerous abortions. Aren't abortions against Sharia Law?"

"No," Sara answered. If a man decides that his wife should have an abortion, then she can. It's not against Sharia Law. "

The panel just looked at me. "Counsel, please address this issue."

"Madame Chair," I began, abortion is not against Sharia law. The issue in Sara's claim is her right to have control over her own reproductive abilities, her right to decide for herself whether or not she wants an abortion. In her case, she did not.

However, her husband compelled her to do so, against her will. This was part of the abuse, the control he exercised over her. She could not control her own body, her right to carry her own babies to term."

"I see. Now, counsel, I want you to question Sara on the issue of re-availment. I understand that she left her marital home and stayed with her father for some time. Why did she return home to an abusive husband?"

I looked at Sara and simply put the question to her, "You had the opportunity to leave an abusive home. What made you return?"

"My children. When I went to my home to visit them, I could see that they were depressed and neglected. Their grades went down. The house was a mess. They had to cook for themselves. My husband was neglecting them. His second wife was neglecting them. In fact, she hated them and that was clear to them. So, I felt I had no choice, but to return so that I could take care of my own children."

The panel member appeared to ponder her answer for quite some time. Then she asked, "But, Mrs. F, you returned at your own peril. You knew your husband would abuse you again, so why would you sacrifice your own safety in this manner when your father had offered you his home?"

Sara did not understand the meaning of the word, "peril" and so, I asked the interpreter to translate for her. He did so.

Sara did not hesitate after the translation. She stated, "A mother will do anything for her children, even get beaten up."

At first the panel member painted an expression of incredulity on the canvass of her countenance. Then, as suddenly as the stroke of a brush her expression changed. She replied, "I find your explanation credible with respect to the role of motherhood in your culture and religion. However, I am having difficulty comprehending the following: "What was the last straw for you? In other words, why did you finally leave and flee to Canada? I understand you left your four boys behind, correct?"

Of course, at this point the interpreter was required to translate the meaning of the idiom – "What was the last straw for you?" I could discern he himself was having difficulty translating this cliché, and so I attempted to assist him,

"You know, the cliché is akin to, "What was the last straw which broke the camel's back?"

"Ohhhh", he laughed, as did everyone in the hearings room, including the panel member, who tried not to, but nonetheless, her reserved laughter made her more human. This really helped Sara, who then responded,

"I had no choice. I had to leave my children behind. My husband wouldn't allow them to leave Saudi with me. I needed his permission and he wouldn't give it. I left because I couldn't take it anymore. If I didn't leave at that point, I would have died. The abuse was affecting my health too much. I thought it was better for my children for me to leave because at least then, they would still have a mother, even if I am far away. I hope to bring them here to Canada if I can."

"I see."

Sara carried on with her testimony. There were times when she did break down and cry. No one could blame her. The panel member interceded whenever she desired clarification or had a question. She was thorough, tough, but fair. Additionally, she was hard to read. This particular panel member usually adopted a poker face, which is professional, but emotionally difficult for Sara. After three and a half hours, she commented, "Counsel, we shall take a 15 minute break, after which I will render my decision orally."

We all rose for the panel member to leave. Sara and her supporters shot a myriad of questions simultaneously, "What's going on? What does this mean? Is it a good sign? Will she give her decision today? Do you think you won? What happens next? Can she bring her children? Can you help her with that?"

I told myself to just breathe. Frankly, this claim put a great deal of pressure on me. I genuinely cared about Sara and her future. Nonetheless, she was a Legal Aid client and I lost money in representing her. Further, the Women's Group was well-intentioned and I respected them, but I don't think they realized the degree of added stress they were placing on me. I felt as if I was responsible for Sara's life, and that is a tremendous responsibility. Of course, I couldn't articulate any of this. So, I tried to remain calm in this panic-stricken atmosphere. I looked at Sara, and stated,

"The panel member will give her decision today when she returns. I don't know the outcome. I can't guarantee I will win your claim. However, for whatever it's worth, I do have a good feeling about your claim. I have a good feeling about the way in which you testified today. You told your story sincerely, truthfully, and I think the panel knows this. How do you feel, Sara?"

"I feel like throwing up."

We all looked at her with sympathy. This poor woman had been through so much abuse at the hands of her husband. She had been so badly abused that she left her own children. Surely, she deserves a safe haven. One of the women asked me, "So, why did the judge keep asking Sara about returning to her husband? I mean, doesn't she realize battered women do that: they get beat up, they leave, and then they return. It's a vicious cycle. You should explain that to the judge."

"I did. I provided voluminous objective evidence about battered women, including the fact that it's common for battered women to leave and return to the men who abuse them. Eventually, the fortunate ones leave for good. The panel member has all that material. Look, this is everything I provided to her a long time ago. So, try to relax. I know this is difficult, but it's a process, and it takes time."

The women were satisfied after I showed them the objective evidence I had provided the panel member. Shortly thereafter, the panel member returned to the hearings room. I tried to read her expression, but it was inscrutable. She commenced her oral decision with a recitation of the facts, and it was in this recitation that I knew we had won. I knew immediately. However, in an abundance of caution, I didn't want to share my exuberance with Sara – what if I was wrong? I didn't want to disappoint her.

After a lengthy oral delivery, the panel member finally spoke the magic words, "Therefore, based on the subjective, as well as the objective evidence, I find Mrs. Sara F a deemed convention refugee. Good luck, Mrs. F."

I was thrilled, but reserved. The women were thrilled and not at all reserved. They ran to Sara and hugged her. The chorus sang, "You can stay, Sara. You don't have to go back." Sara appeared stunned. She had waited for so long to have this hearing, that the decision was surreal for her. She looked at me for confirmation,

"I can stay?"

"Yes, Sara, you can stay in Canada forever. You're a deemed convention refugee now."

One woman stated, "Oh, thank God, thank-you so much. You did a great job. Now, Sara can really begin to heal from the domestic violence. Now, she can start her life all over again. She can find a better job. But, what about her children"? Is there a way of bringing over her children now?"

I looked at Sara. She seemed tremendously relieved. I was happy for her. Then, I explained, the next step is the Application for Permanent Residence as a Deemed Convention Refugee. This takes time to process and finalize. However, Sara, you may include your children in this application. That doesn't mean they will be allowed to come. You have to factor in the laws in Saudi Arabia regarding exit visas for your children, custody issues, after all you're still married to your husband, your husband's position with respect to relinquishing his parental rights, and so on. It's complicated, Sara; however, if you want me to try, I will."

Sara looked at me, and said, "Yes, try, but do I have to pay, or will the government pay?"

"There are process fees for you and your four children you must pay. The government will not pay them, Sara. Legal Aid doesn't cover these types of applications either."

Sara looked to the women. One of them stated, "Our group doesn't have the resources to assist Sara financially."

"I understand," I replied.

Then, the group looked at me. Against my better judgment, I replied, "O.K. O.K., I'll do this pro bono, but I can't cover the process fees, just so we're clear." My response was entirely emotionally because I knew the time, effort and costs involved in Applications for Permanent Residence as Deemed Convention Refugees. These types of applications can go on for years and years and years. They are labor intensive and clients are extremely stressed during the process times. I don't blame them; however, it puts a burden on me and my assistant. Clients will call frequently with the same question, "Why is it taking so long? Why is it taking so long?"

In any event, after the hearing, everyone was happy. All of us did go out for a celebratory dinner. It was a time to relax, take it all in, and rejoice. I took the evening train back to Windsor. I was exhausted, but elated. It was difficult to shut it off, to unwind. I kept playing the events at the hearing over and over again in my mind – until finally, I fell asleep.

Time passed. I completed the Application for Permanent Residence as a Deemed Convention Refugee for Sara, but, as expected, her husband would not permit the children to leave Saudi Arabia. I had no power whatsoever to overcome Saudi Arabian exit and family law legislation. The law was that children could not leave without their father's permission. Sara tried calling her children many times. She informed me that, "They don't want to talk to me anymore. They said I'm a bad woman. I left them to go be a whore in Canada. I lost them."

I felt powerless. I wanted to assist Sara, but there was nothing I could do. I supported her as much as I could, financially and emotionally. In fact, as any Legal Aid Refugee lawyer would know, I lost money. Legal Aid had capped this file at 13 hours for approximately $1200.00 in total. This file went on for approximately two years. When I worked out what I was paid and how many hours I put into this file, I concluded I was paid approximately $5.00 an hour. One should also factor in time away from the office to travel and represent her in Toronto. This means a loss of income during that time. In addition, Legal Aid only covered a portion of expenses, such as accommodation in Toronto.

Moreover, I have permanent disabilities resulting from a serious motor vehicle accident. I was struck in my car by a transport truck which had crossed the highway median. These trips to Toronto were physically taxing given my catastrophic injuries. They rendered me incapacitated for several days afterwards. This all translates to a loss of income. Certainly, it would have been less painful and more cost effective to sit in my office and not take Sara's file or any refugee files for that matter.

So, why do it? Simply, her story moved me, and I wanted to help her. I think all of us have been in a position of vulnerability before, a position wherein we have felt powerless. It's not a good feeling. It doesn't require a great deal of effort to just extend your hand to a fellow human being in need. These helping hands sow together the fabric of humanity.

I would like to say that after the hearing, Sara made a miraculous transformation and her life became a fairy tale, but that's not the way life works, particularly for victims of domestic violence. Sara did find a job, and that was wonderful for her because it was the very first time she had ever worked. However, she was paid minimal wage and the job was far beneath her educational level. Sara had earned a graduate degree in Saudi Arabia, and yet, the only job she could find in a city as large as Toronto was as a cashier in a convenience store.

She still struggled with life in Toronto. There were times when she regressed to the abused woman she once was. During these times, she would only leave her apartment to work and to purchase groceries. I had seen this before. Just because a victim of domestic violence escapes her abuser does not mean she escapes the mindset of an abused victim. This conditioning travels with her. She does not leave her conditioning behind at the airport in her country of origin. Altering the conditioning of an abused victim, altering the internalization of physical and emotional abuse takes time. This change is slow and painstaking.

I had the privilege of witnessing this change. Over time, I began to see the healing process slowly take place. One day, she appeared in my office without an appointment. She was proud of herself, "I drove here all by myself." I smiled, "I'm glad, Sara. I know how difficult that must have been for you." I looked at her deeply, and I could see she was not the same woman I had met years ago. She looked at peace with herself. Her color was healthier, more nourished. She was more spirited and energetic. I asked her, "What are you doing now?"

"I'm still working at that convenience store. But, I feel better. I'm happy now."

"That's progress, Sara."

"Hassan called me last night. His father will let him go. Hiba is pregnant - again. She hates Hassan. She complains to my husband that he gives her a hard time. She can't deal with him. He's too much work. Hassan told me my husband and Hiba fight a lot now. Hiba blames Hassan. So, my husband told him to call me and give me the good news."

"Oh my God, Sara, that's wonderful news. This means your husband will grant his permission for Hassan to obtain the exit visa. Now, he has to grant custody to you, here in Canada. Hassan is only 8 years old, and so who will travel with him to Canada?"

"My husband."

"Oh, are you comfortable with this?"

"I just want Hassan back. You know, it's funny, in the

end, my husband gave me our youngest not because he loves Hassan and knows he needs his mother, his real mother, but because Hassan is trouble for Hiba. Funny, isn't it?"

"Well, no, I don't think it's funny at all, Sara. I think it's sad. Obviously, your husband does not have the best interests of his own child at heart. He wants to get rid of him because Hassan is an annoyance to Hiba, with whom he is having a new family. So, his alliance is shifting. I mean, I know you hate Hiba, but she is a victim, Sara. Your husband married her when she was only a child, 16 years old. He's probably beating her now. You know, Sara, that may be why Hiba is so mean to Hassan. She may be displacing her anger at your husband onto your son. This is common among victims of domestic violence. I feel sorry for Hiba. She's probably suffering, don't you think? "

"No, she's a bitch."

I couldn't help but laugh. Here used to sit a submissive, demure, and covered Muslim woman, and now sits a woman who has the courage to just say it as is. We both laughed.

I didn't ask Sara about her other children as I knew how painful this subject was to her. I knew that her sons had turned against her and hated her. Their father made certain of that. There was no point in reopening this maternal wound.

"Alex, she asked, "Why did you help me so much? I mean the Women's Group told me you didn't make any money. They said you lost money."

"What I lost financially, Sara, I gained spiritually, in my heart. You gave me as much as I gave you."

She looked at me and we had this moment of deep human connection. She asked me, "So, how can I ever repay you?"

"When you pray, Sara, you can ask God to protect my

children. Oh, yes, you can also put in a good word with God when we both meet Him."

She laughed. I laughed. I felt uplifted and fulfilled because laughter is a sign of healing, and it was good to hear Sara laugh so heartily now. That exchange became a crystallized moment of time for me. Sara was now a part of my life - a part of my soul.

Then, I stated, "Let's get back to work. We may need to update your Application for Permanent Residence. Is there anything new you want me to add on your application? Did you move, for example, or are you at the same address? Is there a change in your marital status?"

"No, there's nothing new, except one thing: when I go home now, I'm not afraid of a beating, and I can have a cup of tea in peace."

Postscript

Mohammed, Sara's husband, did travel with Hassan to Canada. Sara, members of the Women's Group and I all met at Pearson International Airport in Toronto. When I first saw Mohammed, I was repulsed. He was dressed like royalty in his ornate Imam garments, with a great deal of gold, pomposity and arrogance. All of us had the same reaction to him. Mohammed approached me first. It was as if he knew who I was. He looked angry, chauvinistic, challenging and threatening. I decided to challenge him right back. So, I attempted to shake his hand because I knew this would disturb him. It is forbidden under Sharia law for a man to shake a woman's hand. And how dare a woman actually make the first move. I thought Mohammed was going to punch me in the face. His face was red inflamed, angry, outraged, dangerous. I looked right back at him. This is not done in his world. Women avert their eyes: they never look a man straight in the eye. The Jewish women were well aware of this. So they circled around me. They were trying to protect me.

It was obvious that Mohammed wanted to punch me in the face, and if we were in Saudi Arabia, he could do so, and get away with it. But he was in Canada now, on our soil, and so our laws applied, only no one knew how Mohammed would react. On the contrary, everyone knew how I would react, if indeed, he did punch me in the face. Quite simply – I would give it right back – but that's another story….

The Dark Sunglasses

ALEX APPEARED AS the typical lady lawyer. I assumed she was a feminist. Aren't all female lawyers feminists? She was professionally attired in a navy blue pin stripped suit, black high heels, although not too high, just enough make-up to enhance her natural beauty, but not overdone, strong, aggressive, bright, confident – a fighter. I could not see her eyes because she had on black designer sunglasses –tres chic.

I met her standing outside the Immigration and Refugee Board on Victoria Street in downtown Toronto. I also practise Immigration and Refugee Law with a major Law Firm in Toronto. We were both obscenely early and the doors to the Board were not yet open. So, we walked across the street and sat in an outdoor patio directly across from the Immigration and Refugee Board. We proceeded to speak shop talk. I asked her, "What type of refugee law do you like the most?" She spoke in a soft, yet passionate voice.

"I love doing gender persecution, including domestic violence, rape, and other crimes against women."

"Wow, that's a labor intensive, time consuming and extremely difficult area of refuge law. I couldn't do it. What made you choose this area?"

"'Well, about ten years ago I represented this poor Muslim Palestinian woman who had been physically and emotionally abused by her husband for thirty years. This woman had six children, all of whom disrespected her because they took their cue from their father. This was the most disturbing aspect of this claim. How could a man turn his own children against their mother? I mean, if children hate their mother, they are bound to hate themselves because mothers are a part of them."

I looked at her and thought, "'Wow, she is insightful because this is so true."

I responded, "Isn't that part of the abuse?"

"Unfortunately, it is. I have heard this same thing from victims of domestic women from all over the world, regardless of their ethnicity, religion, socio-economic class, educational level and the like."

"How is this woman doing now? I assume she is divorced?'

"No, she developed breast cancer as a result of the years of stress she was under due to the abuse. She died a year after I won her case. That's why I chose gender persecution. First, this woman was victimized by her husband, then she was alienated from her children, and finally, she was killed by cancer. Isn't that the ultimate price of abuse? I mean, obviously her husband's abuse had a role to play in the cancer. Cancer is stress related. So, her story made me angry. I decided to channel that anger in helping women in her situation so that they would not end up dead, like she did."

"You know, I never understood why these women just don't divorce like a woman would in Canada. My own mother would send my father to hell for the slightest 'infraction' – you know, like not cleaning up after himself. I can't imagine ever hitting a woman. Why do these men abuse the very women they are supposed to love?"

"'It's multi-factorial. For instance, many of these women are married to Muslim men, and under Sharia law a woman cannot divorce her husband without his consent. Many victims of domestic violence love their husbands despite the fact that they abuse them. These men are not *all* bad: some of them are good and bad. Many women stay for the sake of their children, to provide them with a two parent home. Some stay because they are not financially independent. The vast majority remain in abusive homes because they suffer from low self-esteem, regardless of their positive attributes. I mean, I've represented women who have it all, and still, they live with an abusive spouse. It's a complex and complicated issue."

"But why the hell don't these men divorce their wives? I mean, obviously, they don't love them, and so what is the point of hanging on, of staying in a loveless marriage?"

"Are you speaking from experience?"

"Well, actually, that's very astute of you. I am divorced, and we did fall out of love."

"You sound rational, and that's great. But, in many countries, men of a variety of ethnicities and religions will not grant their wives a divorce because they don't want to free them to re-marry. They don't want their wives, but they also don't want another man to have them. You're a man. You tell me."

"I think that's selfish."

"I agree."

Subsequently, Alex asked me about my work. "What type of refugees do you represent?"

"I represent claimants from all over the world. For example, we represent claimants from Columbia. As you know, the FARC gorilla group is a powerful agent of persecution there. They target individuals, including professionals, who can be of some utilitarian use to them. These people are threatened with their lives if they don't join the group or work for them. Their spouses are threatened, their wives raped, their children abducted. There is a tremendous problem in Columbia with FARC."

"Yes, I am aware of FARC and have dealt with claimants from Columbia. So, you base such claims on membership in a particular social group?"

"Yes, definitely, certain groups of people are targeted by FARC, especially professionals, doctors, dentists, accountants or wealthy business men."

"Yes, I agree with you, but membership in a particular social group is a difficult ground to advocate. You could also proceed under the rubric of a person in need of protection."

"Absolutely, and in an abundance of caution, I do both."

"So do I."

"Do you have a business card?"

"Yes, in fact, I do."

Alex handed me her business card and I was duly impressed with the number of letters behind her name. "Holy cow, Alex. You have a Ph.D.?"

"Yes, you sound surprised."

"Well, actually, I was thinking I will definitely be in touch with you. Our firm is looking for another associate. Are you interested at all?"

"Oh, I'm flattered. Your firm has a great reputation, but I

can't. I have family commitments. However, I am interested in doing some consulting. What do you think?"

"Well, these days, you don't even have to be here in Toronto to work with us. We can use technology to hook up. So, I am definitely going to give you a call. As it is, we do have a vacuum with respect to gender persecution. In one case, a claimant is married and his wife was brutally raped when her husband refused to work for the FARC organization. In light of our conversation, I am thinking, we could pursue gender persecution for her."

"Is she with him in Canada?"

"Yes, she is here with him."

"So, she has her own story. There is definitely gender persecution here. She was raped because she is a woman."

"O.K. Do you have any suggestions regarding the wife and gender persecution?"

"You may make a request to vary the order of questioning so that you can question her first, rather than the Tribunal Officer or the Panel Member. Of course, you do require a letter from a psychiatrist or some other qualified professional to corroborate any trauma she may be experiencing, for instance Post-traumatic stress syndrome. Many victims of rape or sexual assault experience PTSD."

"Seriously? That would help her, but the problem is I don't think this woman will see a psychiatrist. In some countries or cultures, counseling is frowned upon, or not an option for so many reasons."

"Yes, I agree with you. Many women internalize rape, domestic violence or any other form of abuse. Consequently, they feel that somehow it was their fault. So, they will not seek counseling because they are ashamed. Of course, some cultures exacerbate this problem because they condemn the victim, make her feel ashamed. It's a complex issue."

"O.K. I can see that. What about just making the request without corroborating evidence from a psychiatrist?"

"I've done that before. I just state the truth to the panel member. Something like, 'With all due respect, Mr. Chair, or Madame Chair, the claimant is uncomfortable seeking counseling. She and I have a relationship which has spanned a number of years. The claimant is comfortable with me. She is also extremely vulnerable and I would respectfully submit I could elicit her testimony in a gentle, non-adversarial manner without doing further damage to her fragile state of mind.' You know words to that effect."

"No, I don't know. I have no clue about these gender persecution claims. So, will the panel accept this request without evidence?"

"It really depends on the panel. Some panel members do understand this fact, while others require evidence. However, it's still worth trying. All the panel can do is deny your request, but at least you know in your heart that you did your best and put your client's best interests first, right?"

"Right. Right. Well, O.K. Perhaps one day I'll try it, but if the panel yells at me, I am holding you responsible."

Alex laughed. She had a beautiful smile. I think many lawyers are anal; it may be an occupational hazard, but I could not help but think, "Obviously, she had worn braces because her teeth were perfect." She had dimples when she smiled which were adorable. I was attracted to her. She was a beautiful woman. I could have talked to her all day.

"So, is it really worth it, practising in the area of gender persecution, especially domestic violence. For me, it seems like a rather depressing, labor intensive and not so lucrative area of the law."

"You're right on all counts. But, you know, you really can help these women. For instance, so many victims of domestic violence have little if any support from their families and their societies at large. At times, their own fathers condone the abuse because they themselves abuse their own wives. Some fathers do not want the financial responsibility of caring for an adult daughter and her children, despite the fact that they are their grandchildren. There is no state protection because the police consider domestic violence a private family matter and not within their jurisdiction. They have no one to support them. Lawyers are often the only support they have. So, you see, it's fulfilling."

"Well, I admire your commitment to these women. They're lucky to have you. They are probably all poorly educated, never worked and dependant on their husbands."

"You'd be surprised at what kinds of women are abused."

"I doubt an educated, professional, successful woman would put up with it."

She just looked at me.

"Well again, domestic violence happens to all kinds of women, including women who appear to have it all. You see, men who abuse women are systematic and calculating. The abuse occurs over a period. First, they are charming and draw the woman in. Then, they begin to isolate her from her family and friends, from her support network. They denigrate her to the point where she begins to question her own self-worth, regardless of her accomplishments. Unfortunately, I've represented women from all over the world who are professionals, lawyers, doctors and the like, and these women are abused. These women do suffer from low self-esteem."

"I had no idea."

"Oh, here is Dr. Hakim, my expert witness. I'll introduce you to her. You could use her for future claims on gender persecution."

"Thanks, Alex, appreciate it.

Dr. Hakim was petite, brunette, dark complexioned and extremely professional. She wore a designer black pant suit with a crisp white blouse and dark, expensive Versace sunglasses. Alex made the introductions. I proceeded to shake the doctor's hand, but she withdrew. She politely explained that she was a practising Muslim and as such, she was prohibited to shake hands with a man. I was surprised. I mean, Dr. Hakim was obviously well-educated and professional. She was working in Canada, and so I was still confused as to why she would not shake my hand. I shot Alex a questioning look, to which she responded,

"Well, we have to respect a person's faith, as long as it is exercised freely."

It was Alex's turn to shoot Dr. Hakim a probing and questioning look. There was some sort of unspoken conversation going on here, one to which I was not privy.

Nonetheless, the three of us dialogued for a while. Dr. Hakim explained that she had practiced in the area of domestic violence against Muslim women for over a decade. She appeared passionate about her work. Dr. Hakim smiled, was lively and appeared she had it all: however, there was a subtle sadness and fragility about her. I could just sense it. It was nothing vibrant or blatant, but it was very much present in her aura. I wondered what this vibrant, intelligent, professional woman had to be sad about. I was happy I obtained her business card, and I did plan on contacting her. She would make an excellent expert witness for so many of my clients. Her credentials were outstanding: she was a Harvard grad!

"I see the doors are finally open", Alex pierced through my thoughts.

"Yes, shall we go?" I asked.

Alex, Dr. Hakim and I filed through the door to the Immigration and Refugee Board along with throngs of lawyers, clients and staff members. The three of us alighted the elevator together. We were headed to the fourth floor to check in. On the way up, I looked at Dr. Hakim furtively. I could sense she was not the type of woman who would feel comfortable with a man looking at her. She seemed quite shy. The elevator doors opened, and we exited.

It was then that Dr. Hakim took off her dark sunglasses.

It was evident that she had tried to cover it up with make-up. She did a good job. One would have to look at her closely to notice it.

However, I could see her black eye plainly. I looked at her with a silent question mark in my eyes.

She looked down.

It was then that I understood.....

Lies

MY LEGAL ASSISTANT, Hiba, buzzed me on the telephone, "Alex, your 1 o'clock appointment is here. "

"Alright, I'll be right out," I responded.

I left my office in order to meet my client, Mira. She and Hiba were dialoguing and eyeing each other. I looked at the later and instantaneously recognized that thinly disguised "cat-claws" expression in her eyes and in her demeanor. Clearly, and not surprisingly, she disliked my client. Why? Well, Mira was dressed in fitted and revealing attire. She was young, attractive and sexy. It was a gender issue, pure and simple: pretty women are frequently disliked by other women. Personally, I was always kind to attractive women for the simple reason that many of them are stuck between a rock and a hard place: women are jealous of them and therefore hate and alienate them, and men are sexually aroused by them and therefore want to sleep with them - rather than love them – which is what they really need.

"Hello, Mira, it's a pleasure to meet you. Please come in," I greeted her warmly.

She was a diminutive and fragile woman, and these characteristics were reflected in her hesitant and unsteady gait. She held the hand of an equally diminutive and pale young boy, her son. His name was Erjon. My assistant had previously arranged for an Albanian translator, Firas and he was present as well.

The woman was indeed beautiful, but her beauty was scarred by suffering: she had streaked blond hair she wore with style and deeply brown eyes she wore with pain. Indeed, cords of death appeared to have strangulated her eyes. Her son appeared to be approximately eight years of age. He, too, had that strangulated look in his big brown, beautiful eyes. I wondered what he had witnessed with those innocent eyes, and whether his loss of innocence was irreparable.

"How may I assist you today?" I punctured the emotionally intense atmosphere.

"I need to make a refugee claim," she responded.

"Alright, then tell me your story."

"I don't know where to start."

"Well, just begin with your name and date of birth."

Mira relayed her poignant and painful story with the assistance of Firas. At first, she was hesitant. But then, the emotional floodgates opened, and her pain broke into a tsunami of words.

"Well, my name is Mira D. and I was born on April 5, 1977 in a small, concentration camp on the outskirts of Durres, Albania. My parents suffered a lot under the Communist Regime. My dad had to work long hours for food stamps and very little money. My dad worked 10 to 12 hours a day. This put a lot of stress on my father, and he took it out on my mother. He would beat her a lot."

My gaze softened with sympathy for her. Often the eyes

speak more effectively than words. After all, the eyes speak the universal language of compassion.

"This had a huge impact on my life," she continued.

"All I wanted to do was to leave my family. It was a horrible environment for me. I hated seeing my father beat up my mother and I hated to see her take it all the time. I wanted her to stand up to him, just once in her life. I was disappointed in her because she never did. My dad treated her like an animal, slapping, kicking and punching her."

"Excuse me, I apologize Mira, but I don't think Erjon should hear this. He can stay with my assistant."

"Oh, yeh, O.K., sorry - thanks."

Mira appeared so distraught and drained that she could not see the adverse effects her story would have on her young son. After all, she was attesting to the violence Erjon's own grandmother suffered at the hands of his grandfather. Clearly, this is not healthy for a child to hear.

Often abused women remain with their husbands for the sake of their children, but in the end, they can no longer function as mothers because the abuse "hollows" them like an empty and cracked bird egg. Abused mothers inevitably reach a point wherein they have no more life in them. Consequently, they can no longer nurture their own children because to nurture they must be nurtured themselves. They are not: on the contrary, they are emotionally starved and starving.

In any event, Hiba led Erjon into her work area and gave him a coloring book and crayons for his boyish occupation, after which Mira continued her story.

"My mom has grade three elementary education. Her whole life was spent cooking and cleaning for our family and working. She had no joy – none. I never remember hearing my mother laugh or smile. I resented her. I didn't want to be like her. She worked on the government fields harvesting corn and other crops. After that she worked at a chemical factory. My dad would hit her for saying something he didn't like. He would beat her for being five minutes late after a visit with her own sister. He was possessive of her, and she could do nothing without his permission. It was sickening."

"But, Mira," I intervened, "I don't understand - why did you resent your mother? She was a victim of domestic violence. Your father's abuse was not her fault."

"Because when I looked at her, I saw my own future."

"Oh-h-h-h... I understand."

"Anyways, I remember one time my father beat my mother because one of his friends told him she was talking to a man she worked with. I'd try to help my mom by standing in between her and my dad when he'd beat her. But I'd end up getting hit too and he'd threaten me that if I continued to help my mom, he'd beat me too."

"See, my father is a Muslim, and he believes that the best way to control your wife is to beat her. He sees her as his property, and he really thinks he has the right to beat her. Wife beating is allowed in the Qur'an, you know."

"Excuse me." I intervened. "Did you translate Mira's statement correctly?" I asked Firas. "Did Mira actually say that wife beating is permitted in accordance with the Qur'an?"

"Yes, of course", replied Firas. I'm Muslim myself. The Qur'an says wife beating is acceptable."

"So, the Qur'an, the Muslim Holy Book, states that wife beating is perfectly acceptable?" I was incredulous.

"Yes, of course. I mean, I don't beat my wife, but it's permitted in our Holy Book, and many Muslim men beat their wives. It's well known."

"Well, domestic violence crosses all lines, including, religious, ethnic, socio-economic and educational – yes? I mean, wife battery is not limited to Muslim men."

"Well, Mira says wife abuse doesn't happen in Canada."

"Unfortunately, it does. However, domestic violence is illegal here. Wife battery is considered a criminal code offence, an assault. However, let's not get sidetracked. Are you stating that if I research the Qur'an, I will find that wife battery is actually acceptable?"

"More than acceptable,' responded Firas, "men are allowed to beat their wives if they disobey them or even if the men *just* fear they are disobeying them."

"Wait a second – men are permitted to abuse their wives simply if they fear they are disobeying them?"

"Of course."

A pregnant pause ensued as I attempted to absorb and apprehend this perturbing information. Later, I did research this issue in depth. I was aware of the ongoing debate between critics of Islam and Westernized Muslims regarding the issue of wife battery. The critics posit that the Qur'an states a man can beat his wife into submission – a shockingly horrifying statement. On the other hand, Westernized Muslims claim that Islam promotes women's rights and equality between men and women. So, I read the Qur'an to discern what Allah states with respect to violence against women.

Specifically, I examined three translations of Surah 4, Verse 34 of the Qur'an:

Qur'an 4:34 (Pickthall)—Men are in charge of women,

because Allah hath made the one of them to excel the other, and because they spend of their property (for the support of women). So good women are the obedient, guarding in secret what Allah hath guarded. <u>As for those from whom ye fear rebellion, admonish them and banish them to beds apart, and scourge them</u>. Then if they obey you, seek not a way against them. Lo! Allah is ever High Exalted, Great.

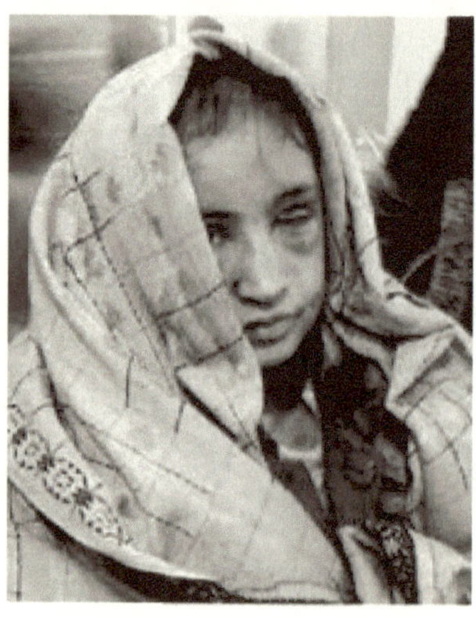

Qur'an 4:34 (Shakir)—Men are the maintainers of women because Allah has made some of them to excel others and because they spend out of their property; the good women are therefore obedient, guarding the unseen as Allah has guarded; <u>and (as to) those on whose part you fear desertion, admonish them, and leave them alone in the sleeping-places and beat them</u>; then if they obey you, do not seek a way against them; surely Allah is High, Great.

Qur'an 4:34 (Ali)—Men are the protectors and maintainers of women, because Allah has given the one more (strength) than the other, and because they support them from their means. Therefore the righteous women are devoutly obedient, and guard in (the husband's) absence what Allah would have them guard. <u>As to those women on whose part ye fear disloyalty and ill-conduct, admonish them (first), (next), refuse to share their beds, (and last) beat them (lightly)</u>; but if they return to obedience, seek not against them means (of annoyance): For Allah is Most High, Great (above you all).

This verse makes it abundantly clear that men are indeed permitted to beat their wives, and to neglect them emotionally and sexually as a form of punishment for allegedly disobeying their husbands in some fashion, even if that "disobedience" proves unfounded.

In other words, a wife does not have to actually disobey her husband in order for him to beat her. He simply needs to *fear* that she is disobeying him in the present or will disobey him in the future ("those women on whose part ye *fear* disloyalty and ill-conduct»). Thus, Allah grants Muslim men the right to beat their wives based on their own subjective feelings and based on subjective future predictions in terms of whether their wives may "disobey" them.

This license to beat a wife is inherently dangerous for obvious reasons: it opens the floodgates for domestic violence. Further, why does a wife have to obey her husband in the first place? Doesn't she have her own mind? The word, "obey" is problematic in and of itself as it connotes a Master/Subordinate type of relationship.

Further, the beating seems to be the final disciplinary measure in a series of increasingly and disturbingly abusive punishments. If a Muslim man fears disobedience from his wife, he should first warn her (that her duty is to obey her husband). If his fear persists, he should subsequently banish her to a separate bed. This is nothing short of emotional and sexual abuse and neglect. Is it also a way of controlling a wife: starve her emotionally and sexually, and eventually she will be compelled to obey her husband – which further begs the question: does "obey" entail allowing a husband to do whatever he wants with a wife in bed as well? In other words, is a wife her husband's sexual slave? Finally, if the husband continues to fear disobedience, he should beat his wife into submission.

It is also noteworthy that Yusuf Ali adds the word "lightly" in parentheses. The word "lightly" is not in the Arabic language of this verse. According to Islam, the Qur'an is perfect and clear. This begs the question: isn't it interesting and problematic that Muslim translators believe that they can "improve" the Qur'an by watering down its teachings? Isn't this simply a form of rhetorical manipulation, a way of obscuring the truth? Doesn't this form of skewing the truth fuel the culture of silence in which abused women live? Doesn't this rhetorical manipulation add one more layer of burka to abused Muslim women?

According to this verse, if a wife "returns to obedience"

(i.e., if the husband's fear of disobedience subsides), the husband should stop punishing her. This suggests that he should continue beating her until he becomes convinced that he has nothing to fear. How long can he beat her? To what extent can he beat her? In Canada, an unconsented touch can constitute an assault. Therefore, if a man slaps his wife, he can be charged and convicted of assault.

Of course, there are a myriad of important ahadith and commentaries about wife-beating; however, it is important to understand what the Qur'an actually states on this subject. Clearly, the Qur'an (which claims to be perfectly clear in its commands) tells Muslims that they should beat rebellious wives (or potentially rebellious wives) into submission, perhaps after warning them and banishing them to separate beds. Hence, as embarrassing as this is to Western Muslims – as it should be - the Qur'an clearly permits men to beat their wives.

I was somewhat flabbergasted and strongly outraged. How can an allegedly holy book possibly condone wife beating? Isn't that an oxymoron: violence is deemed acceptable in an allegedly *holy* book? However, in the spirit of fairness, I also considered the possibility that wife battery may have been acceptable at the time the Qur'an was written, but not anymore.

Mira was incredulous I was even outraged, which spoke volumes about her own psychological indoctrination. She continued her story in a deadpan voice, as if domestic violence is a perfectly "normal" part of life.

"My dad also thought that if I didn't listen to him, he had the right to beat me too especially because I was a girl. He thought my mother's job was to raise me to be submissive."

At this point, I asked for clarification: "So, your father wanted his own daughter to become submissive in character?"

"Yeh, of course."

Again, Mira simply looked at me as if she was stating the obvious, and she could not understand why I was so taken aback.

"But, if your father raises you to be submissive, isn't he simply setting you up to tolerate abuse in the future, from your future husband."

"Well, yeh, so what?"

"It seems to me that a father would want to protect his daughter, yes?"

"Not in my country."

"Right…." I exclaimed in accentuated incredulity. "O.K.… please continue."

"Well, the most important thing to my dad was for me to be a virgin when I got married. This was an honor thing with him, with Muslim fathers in general, ya know. He'd blame my mom for everything wrong we did as kids. He'd beat her if we got bad grades, for example. It was horrible. Not only did my dad abuse my mom, but he also abused his kids - well, no - just us girls."

"Did your father ever accept responsibility for your poor academic performance given the toxic home life he created? Also, it's wrong for him to beat his children, period, but why did he spare his sons?" I questioned.

"Well, no, my dad never once accepted responsibility for anything he did. It was all my mother's fault. She was his punching bag. The reason why he didn't touch my brothers is because he wanted them to grow strong so that their own wives wouldn't control them."

"That is really, truly disturbed. I mean, marriage is about equality, and not domination and violence. To beat one's daughters in order to prepare them to accept abuse at the hands of their future husbands goes against the very essence of parenting, which is love, isn't it? A father is supposed to protect his daughters, after all. To raise one's sons to become future wife batterers is unfathomable."

"Yeh, I remember one time, my aunt said she was happy my cousin married a submissive woman he could control. See, my cousin was a loser, but he felt strong when he got married because he beat up his wife. She couldn't even make a phone call without his permission. And my aunt was happy because now, her son was strong."

"That is parasitic: a weak man becomes "strong" by beating up his wife. Your aunt is morally vacuous: she should be teaching her son to respect and love his wife and not to destroy her — that's real strength in a man. Where are these twisted definitions of male strength coming from, anyway?"

"Our culture, our religion, the way things just are", she replied.

I couldn't help but think that this is the way in which tyranny begins: that is, it begins by twisting the definition of words, such as male strength; femininity; family honor; obedience; and the good wife.

"Anyways," Mira punctured my philosophizing, "when I was in grade three, I remember I didn't do good on a Math test. My mom was very upset with me. She told me I should have studied harder. She told me my dad was going to make her pay for my bad grade and I knew she meant he'd beat her up after dinner. I felt it was all my fault. I felt guilty that I was to blame for what was going to happen to her. I thought that if I killed myself, if I swallowed some aspirin, my dad would feel bad, and he'd be nicer to my mom. So, I took about 40 pills in my bedroom, and washed them down with my brother's secret stash of vodka. I thought I'd be dead by the time my dad got back from work. But I just kept throwing up all night long. My dad thought I had food poisoning. He doesn't even know now what really happened.

"Why didn't you tell him? Did you tell your mother?" I asked.

"No, I didn't tell my mom or dad. There was no point to it. My dad would just blame me, and my mom couldn't help me. She was useless to me. There was no one to turn to, no one at all."

"You have a great deal of misguided anger toward your poor mother. Again, she is the victim here. You should be angry at your father, but not your mother."

"Ya right, and what was I supposed to do with that anger for my dad, tell him, and then get beat up?"

"So, I see, you displaced the anger you felt toward your father onto your mother because if you had expressed the way you truly felt toward your father, he would beat you. However, don't you think you could have been more sympathetic toward your own mother?"

"No, she was weak."

"Wow", was all I said.

Firas intervened at this point and stated, "Well, you know, Alex, Mira's mother should have protected her daughter."

"Firas, what you're doing is re-victimizing the victim: Mira's mother was far too broken to protect anyone, including her own daughter and herself. Don't you see that?"

"Not really", was his response.

I was becoming incrementally annoyed as this interview proceeded. I mean, both Firas and Mira were attacking a woman who was so clearly a victim. However, I was not going to argue this point any further. It would fall on deaf ears. I would have to awaken years and years and years of indoctrination. Nonetheless, as a woman, I felt outraged at the injustice of the way in which women, such as Mira and her mother, are so beaten down and beaten up. After a pause, I asked Mira,

"Did you ever confide in anyone, for instance, in a teacher at school about your father's abuse?"

"No way. I was raised to believe that it's shameful to say anything about your family to anyone. It's a question of honor."

"Is it a question of honor, or is it a way for your father to control and silence you and your mother? I mean, if you cannot speak about the abuse at home, then your father can continue to abuse you and your mother."

"Yeh, I know, but no one really cares there anyways. They wouldn't help me even if they knew about the abuse because it's considered a private family matter, to be resolved at home and not in school or anywhere else."

"But surely your teachers would care about a child living in an abusive environment, and intervene to assist you, or contact the proper authorities, the police, or a social organization along the lines of Children's Aid, yes?"

"No, not in Albania where I lived. There, everyone knows you're being abused, or your mom is being beaten up by your dad, but everyone just stays quiet. No one gets involved. No one really gives a shit."

I sighed…. and then I took a much-needed deep breath. I felt as if I required oxygen. This interview was concurrently heart-wrenching and markedly frustrating. My heart went out to Mira, but I also felt anger at her for belittling her mother so much. However, it is not a lawyer's role to judge, and so I swallowed my mixed emotions and proceeded to state,

"O.K… please continue."

"Well, I have three brothers and two sisters. My brothers treated my sisters and me like my dad treated my mom, with no respect, like we were their slaves. I hated them for this. My brothers were raised to believe that they had to protect our honor. They screened my friends and if my brothers didn't think they were "good girls" I wasn't allowed to be their friend. My older brother grew up to be exactly like my dad. He is 9 years older than me. He and I didn't have a good relationship because I felt I shouldn't have to take orders from my own brother."

"Well, of course not", I laughed, "I mean why would a sister have to take orders from a brother? It's completely inappropriate. Further, it reinforces the patriarchal system whereby females are subordinate to males.

"Yeh, but, I mean, do you have brothers?"

"Yes, I have an older brother as well. I remember, as children, he who would ask me to make his bed, and I would respond, 'Sure, if you pay me.' And he would."

"So, your father didn't get angry at you?"

I laughed again, and then responded, "Where do you think I received the advice to ask for money? If my brother complained my father would say, "Your sister is not your servant. You have two choices: either make the bed yourself or pay your sister to do so.""

"Wow, I can't believe that."

"I am fortunate. I have a father who believes that girls are equal to boys in every sense of the word. I never once believed I could not accomplish as much as my brother. My dad made me feel that I could accomplish anything to which I set my mind. My sister was raised in the same manner. There was no sexism in our home. My dad did as much work around our home as my mom. Both worked inside and outside the home."

"Wow. You're lucky."

"Thank you. But, Mira, in Canada, men and women are indeed equal. They have the same opportunities in terms of education, work and other pursuits. In any event, please continue with your story."

"Well, there was one time in '95 when I was at school my brother saw me talking to my friend's fiancé. My brother was angry I was talking to this boy and so when we got home, he beat me. He said I had dishonored my family. I told him, 'I was just talking.'"

"But he didn't believe me, and said, 'Yeh, all lies, lies, lies. You're a liar and a whore. How stupid do you think I am?' I thought he would kill me. He was very violent with me, and I had bruises all over my body, especially on my neck and face. He almost choked me to death."

"Oh, my God - I am so sorry you had to endure that, Mira. It is truly sickening that your own brother would call you such a foul name, and get away with it."

"Yeh, thanks."

Mira looked into my eyes deeply and piercingly. After a pregnant pause, she said, "Wow, you really care."

"Yes, I really do, Mira."

I knew that Mira had never really had anyone listen to her story before, truly listen, and moreover, truly care. I also knew that Mira had never really had anyone see her before, truly see her. Unfortunately, women who are abused are not even *seen* by those who abuse them. The men who abuse them never really look at them, touch them, see them for who they really are. Nor do these men even care to see their victims because once you look at a person, once you actually see a person, you begin to care, to love that person.

I had heard stories of abuse day in day out for over a decade. There was always this common thread in all the stories I heard, namely these poor women were never truly seen or heard by their abusers. It was as if they were buried beneath a burka of silence, rendered invisible, unseen, unheard. These women were neglected, emotionally mal-nourished, often physically mal-nourished, invalidated - invisible.

I recall one woman who told me her husband never even looked at her when he was intimate with her – never once. She was annihilated by him. He never even looked at her when he spoke to her. If she spoke to him, he would turn his back on her and if she was fortunate, he would respond. However, this was rare. Most of the time, he simply ignored her, and over time, she ignored herself. She internalized the abuse, and this is the point of no return. See, not looking at a woman slowly, but inevitably destroys her. However, the annihilation is not complete until she internalizes the abuse.

I had heard so many voices of Muslim men and women who explained to me that according to Islamic religion, culture and social ethos, Muslim men are not permitted to look at women straight in the eyes because this is regarded as rude and inappropriate. *While accepting different cultures and traditions is all well and good, and in fact, expected within the context of multiculturalism, the fact remains that within the context of marriage, a man should look at his wife, particularly in moments of intimacy because NOT TO is tantamount to emotional neglect and abuse.*

I asked Mira whether any male relative, or husband had ever really looked at her, had ever really heard her. She answered,

"Our men never really see or hear our women. They say it's because men they don't want to be rude, or flirtatious with a woman, but the real reason is - we don't matter."

"That's what I thought. I mean it's one thing not to oogle a woman who isn't related to you, but it's an entirely different thing not to ever see your own wife, isn't it?"

"Yeh."

"Alright, so let's return to your story. What happened after your brother beat you?"

"So, when my dad got home he sided with my brother," she continued. My dad said, 'You're a liar.' He told me I had to finish my school year but after that I wasn't allowed to go to school anymore, or even to go out much at all. I told him I'd quit the next day because I was too embarrassed to go to school with my bruises. My dad told me I had to go to school the next day. He wanted to embarrass me so that I'd learn my lesson and not talk to boys. I recall many incidents in my life where my dad or brothers would treat me like property, and I hated it."

"A few weeks later I met my future husband, Akim. I was 16 years old, and he was 28. He is Muslim. He told me he saw me before, that he knew my brother, and that I came from a good family. He was looking to settle down and get married to a nice girl. I was young and I had never been asked out before. I was flattered by his attention, but now I know how naïve I was. I told him he had to ask my dad for permission if he wanted to marry me. This may seem strange that he asked me to marry him on the first meeting, but in Albania this is the way Muslim men approach Muslim girls. Otherwise, girls wouldn't trust their intentions. So, Akim said he'd talk to my brother first. School ended for Summer Break and then I didn't hear from Akim again until sometime later."

"Then, my dad decided I had to finish my final years of high school at home and take the exams at the end of the semesters. He didn't want me to get into trouble with boys."

"Wait," I interjected, "I'm confused - I thought you stated that your father was upset with you for flirting with your friend's fiancé, not for simply talking to a boy?"

"Well, you see, that's the problem with my father. He never says what he means or means what he says."

"Then, he's the *liar* and not you, Mira. Do you under-stand? He is duplicitous and slippery, and not you. "

"Well, you can't say that to him. All I know is that I always felt confused and off balance, you know what I mean?"

"Yes, I do. If a person never says what they mean, or mean what they say, you can never trust them. So, you feel off bal-ance. This is especially damaging in a father/daughter rela-tionship, right? If you cannot trust your own dad, who can you trust?"

"Exactly – you really do understand. Are you sure you're not Muslim?"

"Yes, I am certain, so go on."

"Anyways, I was depressed and isolated. I missed my friends. I wasn't allowed to have a normal childhood. My dad's goal for me was to marry someone he picked for me and to do it fast so that I would still be a virgin and not dishonor him."

"In July 1995 I met Akim once again. He was charming. He told me he loved me right away. I needed to hear that. But that was a *lie*. Anyways, I saw him as an escape from my father and brothers. I was sick of seeing my mother hit by my dad every single day. I was sick of being kept inside. I was sick of having no life. I felt that my father thought I was "bad", a *liar*, and that is why he kept me at home and didn't allow me to go to school. I felt unloved at home.

Akim and I got engaged in December of '95. He asked my father for my hand in marriage. My dad accepted because he thought Akim and I had already been intimate. I told my dad that we hadn't had sex. Akim and I had met when I was in school, and he would visit me at school – that's all. My father didn't believe me. Again, he said, "*Yeh, all lies, lies, lies.*"

Akim and I were engaged for three years. In the Muslim faith, men and women get engaged and it is like dating in North America. But with Muslims the girl is promised to the man and the result is she will marry him. I had no choice in the matter: once I began engaged, I had to get married.

Akim began hitting me a month and a half after our engagement. He told me he wanted to see if I was a virgin. Otherwise, he would not marry me. So, we were intimate. I didn't bleed and so he accused me of not being a virgin. He hit me in my stomach. He grabbed me by the hair and pulled me to the balcony. He said, 'I'm going to throw you over the balcony if you don't tell me who you slept with, and your dad won't mind.' I told him, 'I haven't been with any man.' But, he didn't believe me and said, "*Yeh, all lies, lies ,lies.*' You know, after a while I began to see myself this way too. I began to question my own character. I thought, 'Well, if everyone is telling me I'm a *liar*, I must be.' Only, I wasn't. Afterwards, he drove me home."

"You must have felt so conflicted: on the one hand, your father, brothers and then fiancé are calling you a *liar;* then you begin to see yourself this way, but you know in your heart that you're not a *liar*."

"Yeh, it was confusing. Anyways, I talked to my mother about what happened with Akim in bed – sorry, I don't mean to be rude, Alex."

"No, you're not being rude. You're being honest. After all, you're not a *liar*."

Mira smiled at me, a smile which extended to her stream-filled eyes.

"Later on, we went to a doctor. The doctor explained that it was normal that you know, I didn't bleed during sex. He examined me and said I had been a virgin. I told Akim and he said he would verify this by seeking a second opinion. Ultimately, Akim told me, 'I'll take your word for it, but I don't trust you. Do you think I'm stupid? Lots of girls just go to a doctor and get all fixed up.'

"Wait a second, Mira – what does that even mean?"

"Oh, in my country, Muslim girls will pay a doctor to repair a broken or whatever hymen so that no one will ever know they're not virgins."

"That's really, really sad."

"Yeh, I know. Most of us can't afford it."

"No, you're missing my point. It's sad that women are so pressured to remain virgins that they feel compelled to pay a doctor to deceive their husbands. It's dishonest and desperate. Moreover, it's a sad commentary on the way in which women are treated in your world."

"I know, but you know what's even more sad?"

"What?"

"It's those women never really know what's real and what's

not real, what's honest and what's dishonest. They never really know where they stand with their husbands."

"Right, so doesn't that make him the *liar,* Mira? When a person never says what he means or means what he says, when a person contradicts himself at every turn, when a person is hypocritical, doesn't that make him disingenuous, duplicitous, deceitful – the very definition of a *liar?*"

Mira laughed, and said, "Yeh, I guess it does. I never thought of it this way. So, Akim is the liar and not me; my dad is the liar and not me; my brother is the liar and not me."

"Now we're making progress!"

She marveled at her moment of epiphany, as did I. It was an "eureka" sort of moment, a break-through, a step toward decompression, detoxing, and healing. Then, when she was ready, Mira continued her story. Years later, she told me, it was the first time anyone had ever waited for her to speak.

"So, during our engagement Akim was abusive a lot. For example, if I plucked my eyebrows, he'd hit me. I had to wear long skirts and dresses which covered me. If I didn't, he'd hit me. The control over me was gradual and over time."

"In 1996 I told my father I didn't want to marry him. I had a nervous breakdown because of the abuse. I tried to kill myself. I took my dad's heart pills, the ones you put under your tongue. I wrote a letter to my mom and my sister. I told them I didn't want to live anymore. I told them Akim didn't love me."

"My sister found me in my room. She told my brother and he and my dad took me to the hospital. They flushed my stomach. The doctor wanted to report the attempted suicide to the police, but my dad bribed him not to. The reason I didn't die is because the pills were old."

"I told my dad I didn't want to marry Akim but he said he'd rather have me dead, and he'd kill me himself, if I didn't go through with the marriage. I told my dad, and he already knew anyways, that Akim trafficked prostitutes, illegal immigrants and drugs. My dad said it wasn't my business and I still had to marry him. You see, my dad benefitted from Akim financially. That was the real reason he wanted me to marry him – money."

"So, again, Mira, who's the real *liar* here, you or your father?"

"My dad. So, in the same year, my fiancé was arrested for carrying a gun. He bribed the judge and got off on a lesser crime. A year later, he killed a young man who was addicted to drugs. He was just 20 years old. I believe Akim killed him over a drug deal gone bad. When I asked Akim if he had killed the poor man, he beat me up. He told me to keep my mouth shut and if I mentioned it again, he'd kill me and no one would find me."

"We got married in November of '98. I was 18 years old. The abuse continued. He was unfaithful. He slept with the women he trafficked. He treated me like the women he trafficked. He would have sex with me by force, and then have a cigarette. When he was done smoking, he would put it out on my private parts."

Waves of nausea overcame me. I struggled not to become sick to my stomach.

"He'd drink a lot. He'd sleep with a gun under his mattress he had so many enemies. He thought I should be submissive, cook, clean, listen to him, have children and be a good Muslim wife. He had no respect for me at all. The marriage was hell, worse than the way I grew up. My husband turned out to be a criminal as well as a wife batterer. He was verbally abusive to me all the time, telling me I was nothing. I was stupid, ugly and no one would ever want me. I stayed because I had no one else to go. My father didn't want me back home. I had no money, no job. Then, I got pregnant with my son. He was born on January 12, 2000."

"I thought my husband would change once he became a father. I thought our baby would bring us closer together. But the abuse continued. I wasn't allowed to go anywhere without his permission. Really, it was no different than when I was a child living at home with my father. My husband is involved in crime, with corrupt politicians, weapons and trafficking women for sex. These corrupt politicians would cover his back. He is very dangerous and has a lot of money."

"I tried going to the police after one of the beatings. This was after my son was born. When Akim found out he beat me even worse. I knew the police had told him. I saw no way out. The beatings were worse when he was drunk. I knew I had to get out or he would kill me."

"In 2001 Akim was arrested for the murder of that young man. But then, he was released after a few months because there was insufficient evidence, but really, he bribed a judge. He was still under investigation after he was released."

"Later, Akim was in the car in front of the house, and he was shot at by men driving by in a car. I was in the house with my son. My husband was not hit as he hid under an outside stairway. Bullets flew by me very close. My son was in the living room on the floor playing so he wasn't hurt. I begged my husband to let us leave to protect our son. I thought our son would be killed by these men who were after my husband. It took time and convincing, a whole year, but in the end, my husband agreed that I could leave with my son. He bought me a fake passport, an Italian one. My son and I left Albania and we came to the United States."

"Then, while in the United States, I made a claim for asylum. It takes a long time in the USA for asylum claims. While in the USA I began to think about changing my life which also meant changing my religion. Islam has only hurt me. I thought about my father and my husband who are both Muslims and all they did in the name of Islam. I was repulsed by all that Islam stood for."

"My interest in Christianity began in Albania when I was 16 or 17 years old. I knew a neighbor who was a Christian and I looked up to her. I read the bible, studied the religion. My neighbor would give me books which I read. Eventually, over a great deal of time and thinking I converted to Christianity while I was in the USA."

"In 2003 I got a divorce from my husband through a lawyer in the USA. My divorce is not recognized in Albania because it's not registered there. I need to be there and do it in person. My husband called me and told me he would never let me go and marry someone else. He'd kill me first. He told me to sleep with one eye open."

"In time, I got married to a wonderful man five years after I came to the USA. I had hired a lawyer for my asylum claim. He told me I should withdraw my claim because if I lost my claim, I would be barred from the USA for 5 to 10 years and then my son and I could not live with my husband and be a family. He said that 90% of asylum claims are denied in the USA. He said that my husband should sponsor me, and I should withdraw my claim so I did and I took a voluntary departure."

"I am scared to death of being returned to Albania. My x husband never accepted the divorce, and he wants me back. I don't want him. I have custody of our son. But if I were forced to return to Albania I know my x husband would kill me, no doubt in my mind. The police would do nothing to protect me. He had connections with the police and corrupt politicians. He is rich and well connected. He has already threatened my family in Albania. He has sent people to harass them and follow them. Their home was broken into. My parents think it was my x husband looking for some clue about where I am."

"Even though he has done all this to my parents my father would not support me if I went back to Albania because he feels I have dishonored my family by getting divorced and leaving my husband. He thinks I must be leading a promiscuous life here in North America. He doesn't even know about my conversion to Christianity. I am too afraid to tell him."

"Akim wants me back. He sees me as his property, and he won't let go. I'm terrified of him. He doesn't want this divorce and doesn't accept it. I am also afraid because I converted to Christianity and x husband and my own family think of Christian women as promiscuous. I wouldn't be allowed to practice my faith – that's for sure. I'm afraid Akim and my own family would kill me."

"I just want to live in Canada now. You know, I love my husband. We've come so far. When we first met and he asked me out, I was so scared. I thought he was going to try to traffic me as a woman. I couldn't believe he was interested in me. Then, over time and a lot of patience, he showed me that he loved me, that I could be loved. It was so healing for me. I just couldn't believe a man could love a woman like he loves me.

He's kind and gentle. He doesn't boss me around or hit me. I love his family. He accepts my son as his own. I just want to stay married to him and live here in Canada."

"I understand", I replied. "I'm happy for you that you finally have someone in your life who truly loves you as you should be loved. I'll do my best to keep you and your son here where you're safe."

Numerous years later, Mira, her son, her current husband and his family all met with me in Toronto for the refugee hearing. There was so much at stake: the future of Mira, her new family, and moreover, the future of a young boy. If I lost this claim, this poor child would be deported back to Albania, and likely, he would follow in his father's footsteps, and lead a life of trafficking women, murder and other violent crimes. Mira's current husband had a lot to lose as well, as did his family. It seemed as though everyone genuinely cared about Mira and treated her as their daughter.

To be honest, this put a great deal of pressure on me as a lawyer. The atmosphere in the hearings room was extremely tense on that day. The panel member grilled Mira for hours about her refugee story. He assessed her reactions to his questions, her gestures, expressions and demeanor. He was trying to "read" her. At one point during the hearing, the panel member asked Mira an odd and ostensibly irrelevant question, "Do you hate your father?" Mira responded, "I can't just hate my father. He's my father. So, I do love him, but I also hate him." The panel member looked at Mira for a long time, and then he slowly nodded in approval. This was a straightforward and honest answer. Children who are abused by their parents, or who witness abuse of a parent, still love the abusers, but they hate them as well.

Credibility is a major issue in refugee law, indeed in law in general. Credibility entails a myriad of factors, such as: is the refugee claimant consistent in his or her story? Is he or she testifying in a straightforward and forthright manner? Is he or she embellishing the claim in any manner? Is he or she appropriately emotional? Has he or she contradicted him or herself? Contradictions which occur in the hearings room are usually interpreted to mean the individual is not telling the truth. However, life itself does not occur in a court of law. If we are honest with ourselves, we would acknowledge that life is full of major contradictions: we may love at the same time we hate; abused women may love and fear their abusers; abused children both love and hate their abusive parents. These are not rhetorical oxymorons; these are the essence of life.

The panel member could have drawn an adverse inference with respect to Mira's credibility, after all, in law, she did contradict herself. How can she both love and hate her own father? A court of law favors pat and simple answers. But the stage of life does not.

In the end, the panel member did not really use the law to analyze Mira: he used his sense of humanity. He was sufficiently sensitive and intelligent to realize that life is complex and complicated, and that what may appear as a *lie* in law is not truly a *lie* in life.

The Lady Lawyer

OUR RELATIONSHIP COMMENCED in a curious fashion: she had appeared before me at the Immigration and Refugee Board ten years ago. Her name is Alex and she is an Immigration and Refugee Lawyer. What struck me most about this young lady lawyer is that she had tears in her eyes when her client was testifying about her refugee claim, about the physical and emotional abuse her client had suffered at the hands of her spouse. They were not false tears: they were poignantly and painfully genuine.

Yet, her pain seemed to spring from something deep within her, some pain she had learned to immure but kept surfacing like poison. As a panel member at the Immigration and Refugee Board for numerous years, I can honestly say that I had never witnessed such authentic empathy from a lawyer toward her client – NEVER. Without question, Alex was sincere, and beautiful – which further drew me to her.

What happened to this lady lawyer to render her so vulnerable, so deeply scarred, and yet, so passionate about her advocacy for victims of domestic violence? I could not figure her out. Alex was indeed an enigma. I tried to speak with her after our hearings, and yet, as strong as she was about advocating on behalf of her female clients, she was reticent and guarded about her own personal life. Of course, this was part of her consummate professionalism: she was very inch a lady – reserved, polite, nurturing, strong, passionate and proper. I thought perhaps this was the reason for her reserve and reticence when it came to any discussions about her personal life.

Certainly, her eyes light up like Christmas stars whenever she spoke of her children. However, other than her children, she never discussed her personal life. Alex always presented as picture perfect: well-groomed, well-dressed and well-mannered, but the pain in her eyes was obvious as much as she tried to hide it. Something was very wrong in her life. I so wanted to help her, but she would not let me in.

One day we were immersed in a lengthy and complicated hearing about gender persecution, in this particular claim, domestic violence. I asked her client, Mrs. Mahmoudi, "Why did you return to your husband in Syria in 2005 when you came to Canada on a Visitor's Visa? You came to visit your daughter – what's her name?"

Here, Alex assisted. Mr. Chair, Farah's daughter's name is Fadwa. It's in evidence, namely on the Personal Information Form."

"Yes, yes. In any event, Mrs. Mahmoudi, you could and should have made your refugee claim then. You testified earlier that the abuse had been ongoing throughout your marriage. You had the opportunity to free yourself of the abuse, and yet you returned home. I need to understand why? "

Of course, Alex interceded, as I expected. She stated, "Mr. Chair, with all due respect, that is a compound question. Perhaps you could break it down for Farah."

"Go ahead, counsel, do the honors, break it down for me."
I admired her spirit and spunk. She had chutzpah, no doubt.

"Thank you, Mr. Chair. Farah, why did you return to Syria in 2005 when you were visiting your daughter, Fadwa, here in Windsor?" It occurred to me that it wasn't Alex's questions which reassured her clients, it was the tone of her voice: soft, kind, humane and nurturing.

"My son-in-law didn't want me in his home. It was causing lots of problems for my daughter.

"What kinds of problems, Farah?"

"My daughter and son-in-law felt they were stuck in the middle between me and my husband. My son-in-law was embarrassed I was talking about the abuse. He thought it was 'haram'. My daughter sided with him."

Here I interjected, "What does 'haram' mean? In all honesty, I thought she had said, 'harem' as in more than one wife or sexual partner.

"It means shameful, Mr. Chair", Alex responded. She smiled because she had read my mind. She had this uncanny ability to do so. I smiled too. After all, these types of claims are emotionally draining, for the claimant and for Alex herself. I could see that. So, it was healthy that she and I could share a reprieve, a private and respectful moment to see the humor in the darkest of moments. It would save Alex in the end.

"I see. So, why is it shameful for you to confide in your own daughter and son-in-law about the abuse you were suffering at the hands of your husband? They are your family. Aren't they supposed to support you? "

Mrs. Mahmoudi answered, "A good Muslim wife isn't supposed to dishonor her husband and family by talking about family secrets, like beatings. It's considered disloyal in Syria."

"I see", I responded, "So, what happened next?"

"Well, my husband called my daughter and son-in-law, and said I was crazy. I was making everything up. There was no abuse."

Alex interceded, and asked, "Mr. Chair, may I continue with my line of questioning?"

"Certainly, counsel, you may proceed."

"Thank you, Mr. Chair. But, Farah, didn't your daughter witness the abuse?"

Here, I interjected, "Counsel, you're leading your client."

"Yes, my apologies, Mr. Chair. Farah, did you tell anyone about the abuse?"

"I didn't need to tell anyone. My children saw my husband beat me and put me down all the time. That's why my daughter, Fadwa, left Syria. She married her husband to get away from her father and the beatings."

"So, why wouldn't your own daughter support you back in 2005 to remain in Canada under her protection, and away from your husband?"

"Because she sided with her father. Her father turned her against me. He brainwashed her. He told her I was lying, and just causing problems for everyone."

"But, Farah, your own daughter witnessed the abuse when she was a child. So, why would she believe your husband in 2005?"

"Because it was causing too many problems with her own husband."

"I see. So, what happened in 2005 when you returned to Lebanon?"

"Well, my husband picked me up from the airport with his mut'ah."

"Please explain to the Board what a mut'ah is."

"A mut'ah is like a temporary wife. You know, my husband liked this young woman, Fatima, but he didn't want to marry her because then, he'd have to support her. So, he and Fatima entered into a temporary marriage and then they were allowed to have sex, like under Sharia law. After my husband was through with her, he just walked away. It's legal."

Here I interjected. "So, just to clarify: a mut'ah is a legal way for a man to have sex with a woman who is not his wife, under the umbrella of matrimony, albeit temporary, and then he walks away – no strings attached, no alimony and the like."

The claimant responded, "Yes."

"Counsel, did you provide any objective proof of this mut'ah?"

"Yes, of course, Mr. Chair. I would direct you to Exhibits 6 and 7. The documentary evidence states clearly that the mut'ah is a legal contract between a Muslim man and woman. It is a temporary arrangement and does not constitute marriage in the sense that there are no legal ramifications as a result of this arrangement, for instance, there is no expectation of alimony and the like. Exhibit 7 is an Affidavit from Farah's sister, Najwa which clearly states that in 2005, she met Fatima, the temporary wife, and this arrangement had detrimental effects on her sister, my client. The affidavit is duly sworn and notarized and we provided you with the original at the commencement of the hearing."

"Yes, yes. I see it. Thank you, counsel. Now, Mrs. Mahmoudi, what was your reaction to this temporary wife?"

"Well, what could I say? I was upset, of course. But that made things worse. My husband beat me up because I was angry about this other woman."

I interceded again. "Mrs. Mahmoudi, that doesn't make sense to me. Your husband was committing adultery, and yet, he had the audacity to beat you for expressing your understandable anger?"

"Yes, that's the way it is in Syria. Muslim men have all the power, not the women."

"But, here he's controlling your anger."

Alex was chomping at the bid. "Precisely, Mr. Chair, that's what abusive men do. They control a woman's emotion, including her anger – which is considered unfeminine. Abusive men beat and damage their wives; however, their wives are not permitted to express their genuine emotions arising from that abuse. They are not permitted to react. Isn't this the most effective way of controlling a woman – it's mind control, almost cult-like mind control. Control and suppress her reactions, emotions, thoughts, actions and decisions, and then isolate her from family and friends, turn people against her, including her own children, and the poor woman is rendered a prisoner, psychologically and physically, in her own head and in her own home. The jailer and warden is her husband."

I just looked at Alex for a long, long, long time. I thought, "Is she speaking from personal experience? Or, is she simply an outstanding advocate for women's rights, particularly for abused women's rights? No question, she was an educated, qualified, strong, intelligent and well –prepared advocate. But, there was something in her eyes which troubled me. I couldn't figure it out. It would take me years to finally 'read' that expression in her eyes.

Of course, Alex never missed a beat, and so she punctured my thought process with her question,

"Mr. Chair, would you like me to continue questioning Farah?"

Alex always tried to move things along for the benefit of her clients. She consistently argued that any further delays in hearings would have a detrimental effect on her clients' need for closure. She was correct. The Immigration and Refugee Board was backed up, and the scheduling of hearings took years.

I responded, "Yes, yes, of course. Please continue, counsel."

"Now, Farah, what happened next?"

"Well, my husband brought me home, and then he went out with his temporary wife. They had sex, I'm sure. Then, he came home to me. He asked me for his dinner. I was really upset. I told him I didn't make any. So, he beat me badly that night. The kids were upset too. In the morning, I decided to go to the police. But, they wouldn't help me. They wouldn't take down a report, or anything."

"What did the police say to you?" Alex asked.

"They said I should go home and be a good wife. It was my fault he beat me up. I didn't look that bad anyways, they said. I should have made dinner for my husband. It was my duty."

"Farah, did you tell the police about the temporary wife?"

"Yes, I did and they said it's only for a few days. He'll come back to you. All men go through something like this. It's nothing. He doesn't love her. So, just go home and relax, make dinner for your husband, and be nice to him. Then, you know, he'll come back to you, if you're nice – like that."

"So, let me understand, Farah. The police informed you that the extra-marital affair, the adultery, was essentially your fault because you were not a good wife to your husband, i.e., you did not make him dinner on the night he had sex with his girlfriend. The police failed to file a report, and they failed to protect you from your abusive husband?"

I had to chuckle, not because I thought any of this was humorous – far from it – but because Alex had this way of piercing through the pretense and hypocrisy of Muslim rhetoric, and calling things as they are, and not as they are presented. She was correct: the sexual relationship with a "temporary wife" does constitute an extra-marital affair and adultery regardless of the rhetorical language.

Farah continued, "Yes, that's the way it is in Syria. The police think the beatings are private things between a man and his wife. They don't take down reports. They don't help the women. They blame us too, just like the husbands blame the wives. It's everywhere in Syria – you know, it's common for a man to hit his wife – no big deal, really.""

At this point, I interjected, "Did the police take any photographs of you, as evidence of the beating?"

"No, they said it wasn't that bad, and then they laughed, like they were making fun of me."

Here, counsel interceded, "Farah, let me understand. The police were cruel and insensitive toward you. Not only did they fail to assist you, in taking photographs of your injuries, in failing to file a report, but they mocked you for having the courage to seek assistance. Do you know of any other women who experienced the same treatment from the police? Mr. Chair, I am alluding to the doctrine of 'Similarly Situated People.'"

"Good point, counsel, proceed', I replied. Alex was correct: the doctrine of 'Similarly Situated People' was indeed relevant.

Farah stated, "Yes, my sister, cousins and neighbors all

experienced the same thing with the police, and we never went back to them. There was no point. Many of them were beating up their own wives anyways, so why would they help us? Anyways, that's the way it is in Syria – the men, they never stand behind the woman to help her. We're alone."

"I see. Farah, what about the women in Syria, do they support each other with respect to domestic violence? Do they offer each other comfort?"

"No, the women have no power. They just shut up and take it. It's shameful to talk about the beatings, even with other women."

I asked, "Mrs. Mahmoudi, are you saying that there is no such thing as female solidarity in Syria – and by that I mean, women do not stick together in order to form a support network?"

"With all due respect, Mr. Chair, may I rephrase your question in simpler language? Farah does not comprehend sophisticated English."

"Yes, yes, of course, counsel."

"Farah, do other women in Syria, women who also are beaten up by their husbands, do they support each other?"

"No way. No way. The opposite – like I said before, we're not allowed to talk about the beatings. It's haram. Also, women don't stick together in Syria. They see each other as rivals for the men. They compete for husbands. They are jealous of each other too. They don't talk about the abuse because it also makes them look bad. You know, the husband must not love them, and so they're losers, like."

"Counsel, I fail to understand that explanation. It makes no sense to me whatsoever. Please ask your client for clarification."

"Of course, Mr. Chair. Farah, try to explain to the judge

why women in Syria turn on each other, why they don't support each other."

"Well, we're not brought up to support each other. We're brought up to hate other women because we all want to get married. Then, when a woman gets beaten up by her husband, it's her fault, so she covers it up. Other women will say, 'she must have done something to deserve the beatings.' Even if a husband has a mut'ah, other women say, 'well, she must not satisfy him. She's cold to him.' It's always a woman's fault, no matter what happens to her. It's all her fault. Even if a woman gets raped, she must have worn sleazy clothes or something. Muslim women in Syria are never ever right."

Alex and I exchanged a look of complete understanding and empathy. As a Jewish man, I understood the abuse and control Muslim men have over their wives. I had seen it time and time again as a Panel Member at the Immigration and Refugee Board. Certainly, this area of law was Alex's passion, her purpose, her mission. This was abundantly clear; what was not clear was *why*.

Alex interjected, "So, Farah, what happened next?"

"Well, my husband found out I went to the police. He was really mad. He shouted at me that I dishonored him and the family. He told me now our daughters wouldn't get married because no man would go near them, with such a mother as me. He said, 'What man will accept our daughters now when they know their mother has a big mouth?' I told him, 'I don't want my daughters to have the same kind of husband as you. Do you think I want to see a man beat up my daughters?' He said, 'You're crazy. I never touched you.'"

"My husband always lied. He always denied he beat me. But I had bruises and marks all over my body. Then, after he denied beating me in the first place, he would beat me again. After I went to the police, my husband kicked me in the stomach, slapped and punched me in the face over and over again, you know – all that stuff, like the usual. Then, he called the police to take me away. My husband made a disobedience case against me. So, the police came to the house and took me to jail for bad women, you know, for women who disobey their husbands, fathers, like that."

"Farah, please explain to the panel member, what is this house for bad women?"

"What's the panel member?" asked Mrs. Mahmoudi.

Alex never skipped a beat. "You would call him a 'judge', Farah, but the correct term is 'Panel Member.'"

I had to chuckle. To be honest, my vanity preferred Mrs. Mahmoudi's title, but Alex was correct – of course. I am not a judge – far from it. I am simply a Panel Member of the Immigration and Refugee Board. Alex was always so prim and proper, but there was an underlying joie de vivre about her, a passion, and a spark – after all, she is of Italian descent. I could see that Italian side of her, and it was unfortunate that spark did not surface more often because it appeared true to her nature. In any event, Mrs. Mahmoudi explained the definition of "this house for bad women."

"It's a jail where bad Muslim women have to go to when they're bad. So, your husband has to make a disobedience claim, like that, and he gets to send you there to punish you for whatever you did to disobey him. You have to stay there until the judge says it's O.K. to let you out. It's, you know, a jail for Muslim women, but not for crimes, just for disobeying your husband, like."

I decided to seek clarification on this point. "Mrs. Mahmoudi, are you suggesting that there is a jail which imprisons women for moral transgressions, or perceived moral transgressions against their husband, as you said, for 'disobeying their husbands'?"

Of course, Alex interjected. "Mr. Chair, I would direct you to Exhibit 10: this is documentary evidence about this jail for women. Muslim women who disobey their husbands are sent to this jail and they are not free to leave until they complete their term of imprisonment. Their husbands must be satisfied that they will obey them. This jail is not intended for crimes; it is intended for social transgressions, for acting in opposition to social norms, for disobeying their husbands, fathers or other male guardians of these Muslim women."

"Yes, I see the documentary evidence, Exhibit 10."

"Yes, Mr. Chair, and I would point you to paragraph 3 of that exhibit, and I paraphrase: the 'nuahuz' is a rebellion against a husband's authority over his wife within the legal context of marriage. This rebellion constitutes a breach of contract. What is the definition of disobedience? Well, the exhibit lists some examples, including a wife who does not obey her husband when he calls her to his bed whenever he feels like having sex with her; or a wife who leaves her husband's home against his permission. Additionally, I would direct you to Exhibit 11, Mr. Chair. I quote,

'Qur'an 4:34 '... And (as for women) from whom you expect rebellion, admonish her, avoid them in the sleeping place and hit them... Allah is knowing. Great."

"The word, 'rebellion' as noted above refers to disobedience on the part of the wife, a duty she owes to her husband, Mr. Chair."

I could not help but note the sharp air of disapprobation

and moral outrage on the part of Alex, and I shared that reaction myself. The concept that a Muslim woman had to obey her husband, father or other male relative, or guardian, was outrageous and went out with the Dark Ages. Simply put, it was anachronistic. The idea that a woman who allegedly disobeyed her husband, for such things as, not feeling up to having sex with him whenever the hell the mood struck him, was barbaric and animalistic, not to mention, utterly selfish. No wonder so many Muslim women were dissatisfied in bed. The concept of intimacy between a man and woman sets up a power dynamic whereby the man is completely concerned with his own sexual needs, and not at all concerned with his wife's sexual or emotional needs. He actually expects his wife to be sexually available to him whenever he pleases. He does not consider her emotions at the time. He does not consider her needs at the time. Moreover, the wife is said to 'disobey' her husband when she does not give in to this sexual whims. This was completely and utterly outrageous for me.

I struggled to compose my moral outrage, and then I asked Mrs. Mahmoudi,

"How long did you have to stay in jail?"

"I stayed there for three weeks, and then they let me go home."

"I see."

"Now, Mrs. Mahmoudi, how many times would you say your husband hit you?"

"I didn't count."

"I understand that, but give me a rough estimation, every day, three times a week?"

"My husband beat me whenever he felt like it, not every single day, but many times. It all depended on his mood.

Sometimes he would beat me three or four times a week. Sometimes he would beat me three or four times a day. It depended on many things, like when he drank he beat me more."

At this juncture, I shot Alex one of my "There is a contradiction" look, but there was no need to do so. She was on top of this claim.

Alex asked, "Farah, doesn't Islam prohibit the consumption of alcohol? In plain English, Muslims can't drink, correct? Isn't your husband Muslim?"

The claimant responded, "Well, many Muslim men drink. My husband would drink alcohol in a black cup so that no one could tell he was drinking. He thought he was fooling us, that we would think he was just drinking coffee. But, we all knew the truth. My husband, like many men, was Muslim when it suited him – that's all."

"I understand', I replied, and then I asked, 'How long were you married?'"

"Thirty years."

"You are forty-six years of age, correct?"

"Yes."

"So, that means you were married at the age of 16 – counsel, am I doing the Math correctly."

"You are, Mr. Chair. Farah was married at the tender age of 16. Her husband is twenty years older than she."

"How many children do you have, Mrs. Mahmoudi?" I asked.

"Eight kids."

"Now, are any of them in Syria?"

"Yes."

"So, couldn't you live with one of them there in Syria, rather than with your husband?"

"No."

"Why not?"

"Well, they have their own families, their own problems. I have two daughters back home and their husbands wouldn't let me live with them."

"Why not?"

"Because it's considered shameful for me to divorce my husband and live with my daughter. My son-in-law can't afford to keep me. My daughter doesn't want to be stuck between me and her father. She has problems already with her husband. He hits her too."

"Mrs. Mahmoudi, you've stated so many contradictory reasons for why you cannot live with one of your children. You testified it is considered shameful for you; your son-in-law cannot afford to support you; your daughter does not wish to come between you and her father; your daughter has problems of her own in that she too is abused by her spouse. So, which is it?"

"Mr. Chair, I would respectfully submit that these explanations are not contradictions. They are reality. My client has provided you with a rational and reasonable explanation for why she cannot return to Syria and live with one of her children there. Her reasons are multi-factorial, not contradictory, and this is a tremendous difference here under the law with respect to subjective credibility. As Farah has testified, it is regarded as shameful for a woman to be divorced in Syria, particularly a Muslim one. Her son-in-law is indigent, and therefore, cannot support my client. Her daughter is herself a victim of abuse, and as such, she is hardly in a position to offer her mother a great deal of support. She herself is depleted and powerless. This is extremely common for victims of domestic violence. It is a cycle: mothers are abused and then their daughters are abused."

"I understand, counsel, but please leave your oral submissions for the end of the hearing."

"Yes, I apologize."

In truth, I did not mind the clarifications from counsel. I knew Alex was only trying to assist her client, and that her client needed to lean on her. However, the protocol at the hearing calls for counsel to make oral submissions at the end of the hearing, and not during the hearing. Nonetheless, I had always given Alex a great deal of leeway because she was so sincere. In fact, she had yet to learn how to develop that poker face expression lawyers are so good at. Alex wore her heart on her sleeve, and she advocated with heart. There was no pretense about her.

Alex asked, "Now, Farah, please explain the line in your Personal Information Form wherein you state that you were raped by a man in Syria."

"Well, in Syria, Muslim women have to act in a certain way. If they don't they get into a lot of trouble with men. So, one day, I needed to get out of the house. So, I decided to go to the market and buy some groceries. By the time I was done, the bags were heavy. Still, I had to walk home. A neighbor, Nasser, saw me and offered me a ride in his taxi. I shouldn't have taken it, but I was tired and the bags were heavy. Then, he drove me to a remote area on the outskirts of Dier-Ezzor. He raped me."

At this point, I interceded once again, "Excuse me, Mrs. Mahmoudi, but something you said is concerning for me. Why would your neighbor offer you a ride The Lady Lawyer

| 133 in a cab?" This may seem like a trivial question, but I knew that often the devil is in the details. I was testing the claimant's credibility, as I was obliged to do under the law."

"Well, in Syria, people rarely drive. They take taxis instead, and my neighbor was a taxi driver for his job."

I was satisfied with this explanation. It made sense.

"Counsel, please proceed with your line of questioning."

"Farah, did you go to the police to report the rape, and if not, why?"

"No, of course not. It's haram. I can't tell the police I was raped. They would blame me. They wouldn't help me. Plus, in Syria, a good Muslim woman should never accept a ride from a man who is not her relative, like a father, brother or uncle, you know. So, it was my fault."

"Why is it your fault when you were a victim of a crime?"

"Because Muslim women know that when a man who's not your relative, asks to be alone with you, what he's really asking for is sex. It's like an invitation to have sex. That's the way they see it. If a woman accepts, she's like saying O.K. to sex. But, that's not what I meant with Nasser. I was just tired from the heavy grocery bags, and he was my neighbor. So, I never thought he'd rape me. I'm friends with his wife. We had dinner together many times, both families. He's friends with my husband."

"Did you confide in anyone, such as your husband, a doctor or your daughters?"

"Well, when I got home, my husband could see what a mess I was, you know, my clothes were a mess; my hijab was torn. So, he asked me what happened. I told him."

"What was his reaction?"

"Nothing. Nothing at all. He just looked at me, and walked away. He didn't try to comfort me or anything."

"What happened next?"

"Then my husband wanted nothing to do with me in bed. He shunned me. When I asked him why, he said that I was a dirty woman, and that I probably had some disease now. He said he was afraid to catch some dirty disease, and that God was punishing me for being a bad wife."

Alex shot me one of her, "I told you" looks. I knew that look well: it meant that abused women are blamed for the abuse they endure. Whether an abused woman is hit, or raped, or denigrated verbally, the blame is placed squarely on her shoulders, and not where it belongs, on the person abusing her.

I reached a point in the hearing wherein I had heard enough. I was satisfied that Mrs. Farah Mahmoudi was in fact, abused by her husband and by the man who raped her. I was satisfied that the police in Syria did not, and would not protect her. I asked Alex to render her oral submissions after a brief recess.

"Counsel, how much time do you require to gather your thoughts?"

True to form, Alex answered, "I am ready now."

I laughed. She was a trooper. "Well, counsel, I need a coffee break, and so let's resume in 15 minutes."

"Of course, Mr. Chair, as you like. My only concern is that we complete this hearing today as the protracted delays in scheduling have taken a toll on my client, in terms of her physical health and psychological sense of well-being."

"Yes, rest assured, her hearing will be completed today. She will not have to return to Toronto."

"Thank you, Mr. Chair," Alex responded ever polite.

The hearing resumed. Alex was an athlete and her game was tennis. Like a tennis player, she *smashed* each issue succinctly and powerfully. She commenced with a succinct recitation of the Personal Information Form narrative, and then she proceeded to address each issue. She began with the issue of internal flight alternative, or whether or not Mrs. Mahmoudi would be able to live safely in another part of Syria. Next, Alex discussed the issue of credibility, both subjective and objective; state protection, including whether or not the police would assist Mrs. Mahmoudi and other victims of domestic violence. Then, she proceeded to discuss identity; re-availment, or returning to one's country after having successfully fled, and finally, the existence of persecution at the present time should Mrs. Mahmoudi be deported. Alex was compelling, passionate and empathic. Clearly, she knew the law inside and out, but this was not her strength really. Her strength was her transparent sincerity. It was obvious she believed her own client. In this vein, she was able to explain ostensible contradictions in a reasonable and satisfying manner.

At the end of the hearing, I declared that I would give a bench decision. I did not require more time to think about this claim. It was a win — no doubt in my mind. After the hearing, I approached Alex and complimented her on a job well done. "Well," I stated, you certainly pulled the iron out of the fire."

"What do you mean?" Alex asked.

"I mean, the issue of re-availment was concerning to me throughout the hearing. Your client had the opportunity to flee Syria back in 2005, and she did not. Instead, she returned to her abusive husband. But, your explanation was convincing. You are right. Victims of domestic violence frequently return to their abusers before they finally leave once and for all."

"Yes, they do, even in Canada."

"Yes, that's true, but in Canada, there are no jails for women who disobey their husbands."

"Yes, that's true, but there varying forms of imprisonment, aren't there?"

"What do you mean?" I asked. I was puzzled by her cryptic response, as I was by her demeanor. She looked sad, which was surprising given the fact that she had just won a huge claim. She should have been proud of herself, and I told her as much.

"Don't look so sad. You were brilliant. Why the gloomy face?"

"Oh, thank you. I guess I'm just drained. The hearing took a lot out of me. Farah is not just a client for me. I really care about her as a human being. Her story deeply moves me, but it's a double-edged sword in the sense that her story both moves me, and enervates me. I just need time to decompress."

Then, she left quickly, but she also left behind a myriad of questions for me, not about the hearing, but about her. Alex's arguments were convincing, credible and compelling, almost too much so. It was obvious that she had a great deal of compassion for her clients, but she also had empathy for them. I wondered from where this empathy sprang. What was her story? Alex was an expert in conveying her clients' story, but guarded in sharing any information about her own story, her own life. Perhaps she was simply being professional? I didn't really know, but I was curious about her.

What I did know about Alex is she was an accomplished young woman, highly educated, intelligent and beautiful. I knew she was a strong advocate. However, I also sensed a guarded vulnerability about her. I could not stop thinking about this enigma. Alex's strength, namely her sincerity, was also her weakness. To reiterate, she had no poker face: she argued for her clients with heart and sincerity. There was no guile in her. I had to laugh one time when her own incredulity over her client's testimony was written all over her face. I admonished her later, "You know, Alex, you have to learn to adopt that lawyer look, that poker face expression. I can discern when your own client is perhaps being untruthful, not from the client, but from your expressions."

"I know", she said. "Many of my professors in Law School said the same thing to me. I have to work on that."

But, she never quite mastered that poker face expression.

Three months later, Alex appeared before me again at the Immigration and Refugee Board in Toronto. I saw her standing outside of our building just before I entered myself. I greeted her, "Counselor, how are you?"

"Fine, Sir, how are you?"

"Fine, how's life treating you?"

"Fine, and you?"

Both of us were not terribly effective at small talk. So, after a pregnant pause, I just looked at her, really looked at her. Of course, she was uncomfortable, and so, I stopped. Alex was the epitome of etiquette - to a fault. She never seemed to notice that I truly cared about her. She never crossed any professional lines. That is all well and good, but annoying at the same time.

So, I decided to push the envelope as it were.

"So, how's your personal life?"

'Fine', she replied – full stop."

I could discern she felt uncomfortable with my question. However, despite her answer, her face gave her away. I could see raw pain – only I didn't know its source.

Why did I care about her personal life? Well, the truth is I was falling in love with Alex. I had been falling in love with her since the very first day I met her five years ago, only she didn't know it. I knew I couldn't cross that line professionally, but nonetheless, I could not help myself.

I will never forget the first time I met her. Alex was representing a Muslim woman, Mrs. Fannouch, from Lebanon who had endured a history of sexual abuse. The first time her client had been a victim of sexual violence was when she was only 16 years of age. She had been sexually assaulted by a young man in her village. Of course, one of the issues in the case was credibility, for example, I had asked the claimant,

"Why didn't you even deal with your own assault until you were married and had a 16 year old daughter of your own?"

Mrs. Fannouch answered, "I don't really understand it myself, but that's when I started to remember things, like the assault."

At this point, I turned to Alex and asked her to explore this issue further with her client because I was not satisfied with her response.

"Counsel," I began, "the claimant testified that it was only when her own daughter turned 16 that she began to have flashbacks of her own assault. How can this be? I don't find this entirely credible."

Alex looked at me for a long time before she responded. Then, she stated,

"My client, Hannan, was sexually assaulted at the age of 16. She did not receive the type of professional or familial assistance she so desperately required in order to work through the emotional damage and turmoil ensuing from the sexual assault. When her own daughter turned 16, she began to experience anxiety, hyper vigilance over her daughter's safety, over and above what a 'normal' mother would experience. This was because her own daughter's birthday triggered deeply buried memories of the assault and moreover, of her attempted suicide years later. You see, she could not deal with the sexual assault on her own. She had no support whatsoever from her family or professionals. Consequently, she tried to kill herself because she was in so much pain, and desperately needed some help. "

I looked at Alex for a very long time. Again, I had this feeling that she was drawing on personal experience. She looked at me, and seemed to sense that I was trying to 'read' her, and so, she averted her eyes and held them downcast. I felt that her client was telling the truth. I felt that Alex assisted her tremendously with her pain and suffering. However, what I wondered was, who was assisting counsel? It seemed to be a matter of the walking wounded healing the wounded. I felt compassion for this lawyer, not her client because her client had help. I wanted to "save Alex."

After the hearing, I approached Alex. "You've never appeared before me, correct?"

"No, Sir, I have not. This is my first time."

"Yes, I thought so. You're from out of town, yes?"

"Yes, from Windsor, and so is my client."

I tried not to stare at her. I could see she had a wedding ring on her finger, and there was an overall reserve about her, which did not allow for personal questions. She was a consummate professional. I was as well. I was also married — albeit, unhappily.

Our professional relationship continued year after year after year. In all honesty, I did try to get closer to Alex. My wife and I had subsequently divorced, and I was terribly lonely. There was something about Alex which drew me in, a sweet vulnerability, and at the same time, strength of character I had never seen before in my entire life.

Years passed. The unspoken words between Alex and me created a strong bond. I think both of us learned to read between the lines, and just know, something was there between us. I could put a name to that emotion - love. But, I also knew Alex had not vocalized her feelings even to herself. How did I know this? I just did. It was the same way I knew I was in love with this lady lawyer on the very first day I met her.

Then, inevitably but inexplicably, the moment of truth had finally arrived. It was a brisk Autumn Day when Alex appeared before me. She was attired in a professional suit, the colors of which reflected both the season and her spirit: deep earthy browns and rich lively greens. She was scheduled to represent numerous clients before me over the course of four days.

"Are you staying overnight then, counselor?" I asked her after one of our hearings together.

"Yes, Sir", she answered.

"Where are you staying?"

"Just down the street, at the Cambridge Suites, Sir."

Then, a pregnant pause....

"Dinner?" I asked.

Alex just looked at me with those piercing big brown beautiful eyes of hers. She never did say, "Yes."

Her eyes did.

But that's another story....

About the Author

DR. SANDRA SACCUCCI, Ph.D earned her Doctorate from the prestigious University of Toronto, where she also taught. She enjoyed teaching on the university level for numerous years. She has taught a variety of subjects, including English Literature, Legal Writing and Business Law. She is a strong human rights advocate and activist with a particular interest in gender- based persecution, particularly violence against women and children. She earned two Juris Doctors, one USA and the other Canadian. She practised law for over a decade. Finally, Dr. Saccucci is a well published scholar and writer.